CW00394706

Hello, It's God

Jack East

Hello, It's God

Copyright © 2022 Jack East Books

All rights reserved.
ISBN:
978-1-8380987-9-7

Hello, It's God

Contents

Hello, It's God

Foreword

I first met Jack East on the banks of the River Adur in Sussex on a dark and starless night in November while we were both walking our dogs. He approached me from the shadows and said "You have been a part of my life. I have watched you as an actor for the best part of 50 years," an extraordinary introduction which had the twin effect of being instantly gratifying and a little unnerving.

Taking this chance meeting as some kind of a sign, he launched into his theory on God, the universe and everything. The next day he delivered the manuscript which you now hold. I read it and his startling story claims that, after approximately 200,000 years of human existence, the deity which has until now watched over the world with apparent indifference, has finally decided to intervene and to bring divine order.

Jack has woven humour into a book rich in politics and profundity, an easy going, shoot from the hip style allowing easy access to some big questions.

For every Christian, Jew, Muslim, Hindu, Buddhist and the innumerate other wishful thinkers, here is the rapture. An opportunity to ascend to a higher plane of understanding, way beyond the dross, poison and slavery of orthodox or unorthodox religion. All holy faith preys upon the innate human need to understand why we are here. Jesus said "I am the way, the truth and the light, no one comes to the father except through me." All change on that little restriction, the entity has announced itself... God is what you make it. The beginning is nigh.

Peter Firth

ONE
TWO
THREE
FOUR
FIVE
SIX
SEVEN
EIGHT
NINE
TEN
ELEVEN
TWELVE
THIRTEEN
FOURTEEN
FIFTEEN
SIXTEEN
SEVENTEEN
EIGHTEEN
NINETEEN
TWENTY
TWENTY-ONE
TWENTY-TWO
TWENTY-THREE
TWENTY-FOUR

DEDICATION

To my wife and my son.
Thank you for not giving up on me.

And to God.
Without you this book would never be
possible. Enjoy the Pabst.

ACKNOWLEDGEMENTS

A special thank you to Peter, my friend.
Thank you for challenging my ideas.

Also, thank you Mr Hitchens. You saved me from a
logical fallacy. Whatever that is.

I look forward to not meeting you in the afterlife.
But that would be a great party wouldn't it.
The Johny Walker Black Label is on me.

"Copyright © 2022 by Jack East Books

All rights reserved. No part of this publication may be reproduced, distributed, or transmitted in any form or by any means, including photocopying, recording, or other electronic or mechanical methods, without the prior written permission of the publisher, except in the case of brief quotations embodied in critical reviews and certain other non-commercial uses permitted by copyright law. For permission requests, go to the address below.

www.jackeastbooks.com

https://
www.facebook.com/JackEastBooks/

This book is a work of fiction and should be read with that in mind. Characters, places, real people and historical events have been used fictitiously. Other names, characters, places, and incidents are the products of the author's imagination and any resemblance to persons living or dead or places are purely coincidental.

At no point does the author condone or condemn any faith or lack of it.
He would just like to ask a very simple favour.

Think.

If this story really happened,
what would your position be.

But more than that.

Why?

Why is the best question ever.

I know what my why is, what's yours?

ONE

"Hello, let's go to line three and Bill from Denver. You are through to The Godless Debate; what's your question?"

Mark had said the same words for nearly a decade.

At first, he was excited to be hosting his own internet phone-in show and his adrenaline raced when the red broadcast light glowed on his console; but that was a long time ago. Since then, he had dealt with the same religious apologist crap every week and now he was on episode 500.

"Hi Mark. Just so you know, I love the show and you are named after my favourite saint."

Mark sagged in his seat.

Another believer who wanted to explain why a total lack of proof should convince him to abandon logic and welcome "The Lord" back into his life. A choice which religionists preach should be based on faith alone.

"Mark, I'm a little nervous, so bear with me. You have said you are an atheist and that you would welcome God proving to you that he exists. You think The Bible is a complete work of fiction and that faith alone is not the pathway to truth. So my question is, what evidence would you need to accept there is a god that created the universe?"

"Well Bill, first of all, I have no idea what would convince me. I haven't met a god before, so how would I know what would prove one exists.

Secondly, The God in the Bible has some questionable moral standards around genocide, slavery, homosexuality and, more relevant to half the world's population, women's rights. That means he has a lot of explaining to do before anyone like me would want to follow him. Thirdly; even if I met one, how would I know they were 'The One' who was actually the architect of the universe and creator of everything?"

The line went quiet for a few seconds. For a moment, he thought the caller had hung up. Then a calm voice filtered through his earphones. "Mark, you realise that means there is no way God could ever satisfy you he was the one and only true deity unless you personally watched him create the cosmos."

Over the last decade, the host had carefully created a simple challenge that no religious person could ever satisfy. As soon as they came online, he knew they were always on the wrong end of the argument.

Each logical trap he developed had been meticulously prepared and, in the unlikely event someone would get close to cracking his iron-clad reasoning, Mark could always accuse them of a lack of morals based on the bible's stance on slavery and he would hit the button that terminated the call.

His finger hovered over the red 'Call End' button as Bill continued.

"Be honest, Mark. Give me one scenario where God could prove he was real."

"Ok," he said, already at the end of his patience, "if God transports me to the beginning of the universe and lets me watch him or her trigger the big bang, I will start my show next week by admitting I am now a believer and that a deity exists. How's that Bill?"

Everything turned black.

Marks words echoed into the void.

Around him was only darkness. On all sides, he stared into empty, desolate, nothingness. Somehow he was floating in the vacuum of space without any reference points to help orient himself.

As he spun around for the third time, a giant red button appeared in front of him. On the top, in large white letters, it simply said "START".

"Go on, Mark, press it," said a voice behind him.

He twisted around, but, apart from the button, there was no light to see who was talking.

"Who's there? What's happening? Where am I?"

"I thought you just said you wanted me to show you the beginning of the universe?"

Instantly, last nights tequila binge became the probable source of this hallucination, but the voice was not just close; it was inside his head, outside his head, everywhere.

"What? Who..?"

"Perhaps this will help. Let there be light," said the voice.

A tiny glow illuminated Marks hand. In front of him a small man, slightly above five feet high, became visible. The chap wore white robes and sported a silver beard and long grey hair.

"Hello, I'm God, and this is the beginning of the universe. I thought you might like to press the button to kick things off."

For a minute, everything was quiet. Mark turned around a few times to look for hidden cameras. He was half expecting his production team to be hiding in the darkness, ready to jump out and start laughing, but no-one did; in fact, his production crew would not be born for another 13.8 billion years. There were just the two of them, silently, floating in the void.

"So you are God, and you want me to press the big start button on creation?" asked Mark, trying to rub some sense into his head with the ball of his palm.

"Well, actually, that would make you God. The creator of all things. The initiator of the universe. The great architect."

"No but that is you isn't it? I would just be pushing a big red button."

"Yes, you are right. I'm just pulling your leg. I'll sort everything out, but I thought it would be a great cocktail party story for you if I let you press the starter as a symbolic act. Like smashing a bottle of champagne to launch a ship. What do you think?"

Mark rubbed his temple harder, trying to stabilise his spinning head.

"I think I drank way too much tequila last night, and someone slipped some speed in my glass."

A hand rested on his shoulder.

"Mark, I'm God. You wanted proof, and here we are, back at the beginning of time.

Now, please press the button so we can get everything going and be back in time for dinner. What do you say?"

Mark looked at the scarlet button, then at the little man and, after a couple of seconds, back at the button.

He lifted his hand and rested it on the shiny red surface.

"Here goes, I guess."

With slight pressure, it clicked and the universe exploded into being.

Mark watched as the skies turned white, and the great expansion began.

"What do you think," said God.

"I thought it would be louder," said Mark.

"Everyone says that," said God and they both disappeared, leaving the universe racing across the skies behind them.

TWO.

Jeremiah Parmenus had been asleep in his cabin for an hour. As he rolled over, stretching his limbs to wake his body for the day ahead, he started to piece together information that would help him identify his current location. Spending four days a week, every week, on his private jet had messed with his ability to wake up knowing where he was. Next to him, a young woman lay naked under a silk sheet. Yes, he remembered now. Rebecca had climbed aboard the private jet four hours earlier, happy to be chosen to accompany him on his evangelical tour of the midwest. When he first met her three weeks ago, at the Church of the Sacred Heart, she had immediately caught his eye. He was preaching just off Sunset Boulevard, and he had taken his production team to run a live broadcast on the internet featuring his guest appearance at the churches smash show, "The Gift". The two days in Los Angeles had been very profitable. His Christian show had netted him two hundred and fifty thousand dollars plus additional bookings around the country.

Over the years, experience had told him a beautiful young girl like Rebecca would be a welcome bonus to the financial haul he had already made. She was twenty, pale blue eyes, with lightly tanned skin. Her smile had glowed from the second row of the audience and immediately made his bitter heart race with desire. As he built to a crescendo, working steadily towards the end of his sermon, she looked innocently over the heads of the people in front of her and hung on his every word. After the show ended, his personal security director had invited her backstage and made sure she was over eighteen. No reason to go to jail for something as stupid as the statutory rape of a minor. Jeremiah prided himself on being more intelligent than people like Epstein and Weinstein. If he wanted to spend some time with a fourteen-year-old, there were plenty of countries where he could buy that particular treat anonymously and for chump change.

He looked down at Rebecca and he patted himself on his back for choosing this devout life.

During his early years in business, he had struggled to make a living. From penny ha'penny extortion rackets, abandoned blackmail attempts and petty criminal activities, he had scraped a pathetic living. In his old life, beautiful young women like Rebecca would have felt disgust or pity when they walked past him on the street. He had never been blessed with the fine clothes, perfect teeth and full head of hair that would help most people pigeon hole him as handsome. Like his father, his hair had receded at an early age, and his teeth made him look like he had been a victim of the post-war British dental system. Now, all that had changed, and he had God to thank for it. Well, more precisely, God and a T.V. Evangelist called Harvey Willson. The older man had inadvertently convinced Jeremiah that a belief in The Great One would deliver his wildest dreams. This was good because Jeremiah had very wild dreams.

At that time, he was working as an odd job man at a football stadium. In those dark days, before his strategic name change, he was called Jerry. During big games, he regularly boosted his income as a part-time odd job man for the Dallas–Fort Worth metroplex with a little petty theft from their locker rooms. Jerry discovered he could easily sell collectable items on a fledgeling internet site called eBay.

The weekend he met his saviour, the stadium had been hired for a Gospel convention. Harvey Willson was the big draw that day and would be preaching his usual mix of frenzied exultation to a backdrop of stirring harmonies supplied by The Eleventh Commandment gospel choir.

During the first show that day, Jerry had been on maintenance duty and watched as the giant stadium slowly filled with happy clapping morons who spent the afternoon shelling out vast sums of money in the name of donations for Harvey's church. By Jerry's reckoning, the weekend would net Harvey more money than he had seen in a decade.

At the end of the first performance, the audience left with hearts full of Christ and their pockets empty of cash.

Jerry had been chewing through a tasteless hotdog which he had bought from one of the hundred overpriced vendors on-site when his radio suddenly crackled into life. "Jerry, where the hell are you?" His boss' voice barked.

The mention of his name had made him jump to attention, but Jerry waited a few seconds before he replied, just to piss the old guy off.

"Yeah, Dave, what's the problem?"

"The problem is that your expert services are needed in the VIP suite. Apparently, Harvey has managed to block his crapper. Probably with the vast amount of bullshit he was spouting this afternoon. He wants it unblocked immediately so he can take a dump before tonight's performance. Grab your plunger and get your arse over there."

"Will do, boss. Consider it plunged," said Jerry, taking as much time as he could to finish his chilli-dog before he headed to the executive lift which would whisk him to the top floor.

As he exited the elevator, he walked past two massive security guards dressed like Secret Service operatives. They would not have looked out of place standing at the steps of Airforce One. Each gave him the once over as Jerry waved his plunger like it was a gold plated security pass. The guard to his right opened the door and called inside, "Harvey, the guy is here to fix the toilet."

A voice inside shouted something unintelligible and the guard turned back and waved Jerry inside.

He walked into the VIP suite and stopped dead in his tracks. Most of the people in the room were young, female, and looked like super-models. A dozen bottles of vintage Champaign sat chilling in giant silver bowls on stands that had been carefully scattered around the edge of the massive glass booth. A table at the far end was covered with a silver platter that held a whole roasted pig sitting next to a crystal tray of black caviar which had spent the afternoon cooling on a bed of crushed ice.

Standing in the middle of the room was Harvey, dressed in a white suit that positively glowed. He smiled as Jerry walked in. "Fabulous, my friend, you are a sight for my sore arse. One of our lovely ladies, who will remain nameless, has managed to block the toilet with some of her feminine items." Harvey shot a glance sideways at a blonde who immediately blushed scarlet. "Now, if you could extract her elephant-sized tampon from our porcelain facility, it would be marvellous because I feel the call of nature approaching."

Jerry walked past the embarrassed young woman and into the adjoining room where the private toilet was located. He stepped inside the bathroom and approached the problem in question. This was the first time he had been inside a VIP suite and he was amazed to see the opulence lavished on the most basic functions a human could have. In front of him was a gold plated W.C., complete with a handle sculpted to resemble a dolphin. As he lifted the seat, his face was reflected in the mirror-like finish. Inside, the water was rippling just below the rim. Nothing could be seen inside, so he guessed the young lady's item was stuck around the bend. Jerry looked around the room, amazed at its size. It was bigger than his whole apartment. Earlier, he had heard Harvey preaching about generosity, delivering his message that people should look to themselves and give to God so that the evangelist could take his word to the ungodly. "Remember Jesus' words," he had melodically barked over the immense P.A. system. It was so loud it made his words sound like God himself was speaking. "It is easier for a camel to go through the eye of a needle than for a rich man to enter the Kingdom of God". After pausing for dramatic effect, he continued, "Relieve yourself of that burden. Give unto God so that we may better spread his word." As if on cue, hundreds of volunteers started walking along the stands shaking huge white buckets with the words "Remember, God Sees Into Your Hearts And Your Wallets."

Jerry looked down at the golden throne. "I don't think you will be entering the Kingdom of Heaven anytime soon, Harvey. Not carrying all that money." He swung the plunger into the water and, after a couple of hard stabs, the water drained down to its normal level. Two test flushes later, he was satisfied it would be capable of dealing with Harvey's planned visit.

As he was about to open the door to the adjoining room, he heard the preacher's voice. It was raised and angry.

"So where has the cash gone? We are 20% down from last weekend. Are some of the volunteers getting light-fingered and helping themselves?"

"No boss. We warned you before we chose this place. The average income is lower here than in Memphis. People have less cash to spend, and that is reflected in the day's takings."

Harvey's voice flew into a rage, "I couldn't care less if their kids starve to death because they have given me the last ten bucks in their pocket. I've got a final payment to make on a twenty million dollar jet and, unless these rubes shell out the dough tonight, I will have to break into the Cayman Islands funds. That will cost me a fortune in penalties."

Jerry turned the handle and tried to invisibly walk past Harvey and the smartly dressed businessman in front of him.

"Hey you," Harvey said, "what's it like cleaning toilets for a living?"

Jerry stood still like a deer in the headlights.

"I bet it's a shit job, isn't it?" Harvey laughed and turned back to the young man. "And if you don't get the donations back on track tonight, you will find out just how shit it is when I fire you. Unlike the lovely ladies next door, you don't have a tight butt and perky tits to convince me to cut you some slack, now sod off and do your job."

The man ran through the door towards the main exit guarded by the CIA clones.

Harvey turned towards Jerry. "Sorry, I didn't mean to pick on you, but he needed to know where he could end up if he doesn't get his rear in gear. Are you hungry?"

Jerry thought about the tiny hotdog he had eaten and then the sumptuous buffet in the next room. He nodded excitedly.

"Ok," said Harvey, fishing in his pocket, "take this and get yourself a chilli dog as a thank you for fixing the shitter." He pushed two crumpled dollar bills into Jerry's hand and moved him towards the main door.

As he walked past the guards, one of them looked at the money in Jerry's hand. "He's a real philanthropist, isn't he?"

"Oh yeah," said Jerry, "he's all about the common man."

Later that night, Jerry saw the young businessman a few times. Always running around the stadium and continuously shouting at the volunteers. Energetically, he encouraged them to ask for more donations as people turned their pockets out in the name of The Lord and Harvey's new Boeing.

Within a week, Jerry had found God, started his own tax-exempt ministry and began building his personal congregation. The first two years were tough. He had to expose his darker side. Obviously, not all of it. Just enough to show redemption for his earlier sins and make him appear a repentant man who had once fallen from grace, but not enough to expose his contempt for the human race. If the people who attended his services knew he regarded them as walking wallets, they would abandon him along with his bank account, and that would not be acceptable.

In year three, he took four months off. His congregation believed he was in holy contemplation, but in reality, he was having hair plugs, liposuction and his teeth fixed.

When he reappeared, he preached his revelation. God had found him and spoken to him personally. The Lord had touched his hand, and Jerry's body had accepted the glory of creation. It had cleansed his soul and regrown his hair. Hallelujah! Praise be to God who could heal his heart and his hairline.

On his return to his holy cause, he had taken on the name that God had supposedly given him during his visitation. In reality, it was the result of googling holy names beginning with J.

Jeremiah was born, and, over the next decade, he built a super church that generated millions of dollars every year. Not to mention the long string of cute religious chicks that were desperate to fill their body with the power of God. Jeremiah couldn't fill them with the power of the Lord, but he took it on himself to stand in for their deity as often as possible.

He learnt an important lesson early in his ministry, courtesy of his mentor Harvey. One morning he turned on breakfast television to see the old evangelist being handcuffed and fed into the back of a black and white patrol car. Apparently, the old man had decided checking a girl's driving license for her age was too much trouble before taking them to bed. In fact, he had made the same mistake forty-seven times over a five year period, according to the Attorney General who litigated the case.

Since then, Jeremiah's assistant had photographed, catalogued and filed age confirmation for every woman who came into contact with him. "Better safe than sorry," he thought.

Next to him, Rebecca took a deep breath. He watched her chest expand and the silk sheet slide off her breast. He leant over to touch her but changed his mind at the last minute and picked up the T.V. remote from the bedside table.

As he pressed the red button, the huge screen that had been bolted to the opposite wall lit up with a menu of channels. He selected a random news feed. The sound was muted, but a group of people in a small television studio filled the picture. Underneath it, a ticker-tape rolled across the bottom of the panel.

He read the words once. Then again. And finally, he said them out loud. "God kidnaps atheist T.V. host."

Jeremiah turned up the sound so that he could hear it above the gentle hum of the jets engines as an excited young man was halfway through answering the reporter's question.

"...and he disappeared in the middle of a broadcast. Just vanished in front of us." The picture cut to a recording of the host talking to a call-in guest and, in the middle of a heated exchange, he vanished."

Over the film, the reporter said, "...and you want us to believe God kidnapped him? Why do you think the Lord came down to Earth after two thousands years absence, and abducted an atheist T.V. Host?"

The production assistant pointed at a monitor on the desk. In big letters, it said, "Hello, it's God. Mark is coming with me to the beginning of the universe, and then we are going for dinner at Hooters. He'll be back in the morning."

"So," said the reporter, slipping into his best sarcastic voice, "you would like us to believe God sent you this email?"

The young producer looked up from the screen. "It's not an email."

"Ok, a text then."

"It's not a text either."

"Ok, so what media did God use to send this otherworldly message? Is he on Twitter?"

The producer pushed the screen backwards and it fell onto the floor, shattering the screen as it landed. Above the desk, the letters remained floating in the air. He flicked the capital letter G towards the stunned reporter. It bounced off his forehead, swept around in an arc and then returned to its place in the message.

The reporter screamed, dropped his mic and ran for the door.

On his plane, Jeremiah shook Rebecca awake.

"What? What's wrong?"

"Rebecca, honey, we may have a slight problem. Get your clothes on; we need to get back to L.A."

***

Mark looked across the table at the man in front of him. The robes were gone and he was now wearing an England soccer shirt and sweatpants. His hair was shorter, and the beard had been replaced with a neatly trimmed goatee, but it was still the same man who had taken him to the beginning of the universe.

"Are you sure you don't want some of these wings? The sauce is really hot, but the blue cheese calms it down nicely," said God.

"Er, no thanks. You tuck in."

God had already eaten six pieces and was now on his second portion. A very pretty girl, dressed in orange hot pants and a Hooters T-shirt, casually walked over.

"How are the wings?"

God looked up and smiled. "Great thanks, could I have some more blue cheese, please?"

"Of course, Honey," she said, "and what about you?" She looked at Mark and then at the row of empty Budweiser glasses in front of him.

"Yeah please, another couple of beers would be great."

"You sure are thirsty. Had a busy day?"

"Yes, I had to help start the universe, and then we travelled 13.8 billion years to be here. My friend says time travel always makes you dehydrated."

The girl smiled and said, "Well thank you for making an effort and coming all the way to Hooters Miami. We appreciate your custom." She grabbed a handful of empty glasses and headed for the bar.

"Why are we at Hooters, God?"

"Bill."

"What?"

"Call me Bill. God seems very formal."

"I thought you were formal. You know. 'I the LORD thy God am a jealous God, visiting the iniquity of the fathers upon the children unto the third and fourth generation of them that hate me'."

"Who said that?" asked God.

"You did."

"Not me. Sounds like someone throwing a hissy fit. Why do you think I said that?"

"It's in The Bible. Exodus 20:5."

"Not me. Must be some other god."

"Thou shalt have no other gods before me."

"What?"

"You said, 'Thou shalt have no other gods before me'."

"Not me. Let me guess, The Bible again?"

"Well yeah. It's sort of your go-to book, isn't it?"

"I haven't read all of it myself, but I get the impression it's not very accurate."

"So, er, Bill, why are we in Hooters? I would have thought this was more the Devil's place than yours."

God looked up from his dinner. He wiped hot sauce off his fingers and took a long drink from the glass of beer in front of him. "Listen, Mark, you seem to have an unusual opinion of me, which seems strange as we have never met before."

"But The Bible…"

"Yeah I know; the Bible says this, and The Bible says that but it was written two thousand years ago by lots of different people, hardly any of whom had met me. On top of that, many were writing down centuries-old stories that had been passed on verbally. What chance do you think that there is a lot of accuracy inside its covers?"

Mark nodded in agreement and clapped his hands. "I knew it!" he shouted. "That's what I have been saying for years. It is one of the reasons I am an atheist."

"Were."

"Were what?"

"Were an atheist. I assume you believe in me now."

"To be honest, I'm still struggling a bit. Sitting drinking beer in Hooters doesn't help. Sort of makes me believe I am having a psychotic breakdown or something."

God smiled and Mark immediately felt calmer.

"Does that happen all the time when you are around?"

"Does what happen?"

"People are filled with happiness."

"Yes, mostly. It is a side effect of creating the temporal field which enables me to be here. Sort of like a warm and fluffy static shock."

"So why Hooters God? Er, I mean, Bill."

"Best wings in town, and the staff are always very attentive."

"And you drink Budweiser?"

"I prefer Pabst Blue Ribbon, but they don't stock it. More of an honest working man's beer, I think. I like to think of myself as one of the proletariat, after all, I did build the universe."

Mark sat back in his chair and looked around the room. Half of the tables were occupied with a mixture of families and small groups watching the football on the T.V. screens. They were oblivious to God's presence and kept busy laughing as they had a good time. Outside, he could see Miami Bayside and a continuous line of people wandering past. Mark looked back at the little guy in front of him. "Why me?"

"You kept asking to see me. I have tuned into the show a few times since I got back, and you seemed sincere, so I decided what the heck. Let's have a chat."

"You know I have a million questions to ask you."

"Only a million?" said God, flashing a cheeky grin.

The girl with a tray holding two beers arrived. "Here you go, gentlemen," she said and carefully placed them on the table.

"Thank you, Angela," said God.

Angela looked down where her name badge should have been. She must have left it in her bag. She looked deep into the older man's eyes.

"Do you mind me asking? Have I served you before? You look very familiar."

"It's not my first rodeo here, but it is my first time being looked after by you, and, may I say, you are doing a fabulous job."

Mark leaned forward, already slightly buzzed by the beers. "Angela, this is God."

Completely unfazed, she said, "*The* God or *a* god?"

"*The* God," said God. "Unless you know another."

"I have met a lot of men who thought they were God but never the actual one. Pleased to meet you God." She shook his hand. As soon as their fingers touched, she gasped.

"I know," said Mark, "it's a bit unnerving at first, but you get used to the feeling."

Tears welled up in Angela's eyes. "I have always believed. Even when times were hard," she said, clinging onto God's hand.

"I know you did Angela," he said. "Sorry I wasn't around to help, but I'll be here for a while now if you need me."

"Thank you," she said, "I'm ok now; all those times have gone."

"I know they have," he said, "and you will be ok for a long time now."

She wiped away her tears, let go of his hand and headed for the toilet to fix her makeup.

"Nice girl."

"Do you know everything about all of us, Bill?"

"No, but I am very empathic. I feel things about people."

"So, what do you feel about me?"

God leaned back in his chair.

"Mark, I feel you are going to buy me another beer before you start asking your million questions."

"Bill, your feelings are amazingly intuitive." Mark waved at Angela as she emerged from the toilet. He pointed at God's glass and held up two fingers. She nodded and smiled.

A minute later, she arrived with two bottles of Pabst. "We seem to have run out of Bud, but we found a load of PBR in the cooler out back."

"Perfect," said God.

Angela left the bottles and hurried to the next table to take an order.

"Perks of being God?" said Mark looking at the miraculous arrival of Bill's favourite beer.

"It has got to have some benefits, hasn't it," said God as he took a drink from the long neck bottle.

He savoured the taste before setting it back on the table.

"Umm, much better, now, fire away."

THREE

Father Paul had been awake for fifteen hours. Earlier, he had gone to bed at 11.55pm after having dinner with Cardinal Johnson, his direct supervisor at The Vatican, and had only been asleep for twenty minutes when his mobile phone started buzzing. Before he could answer, the landline began ringing in the next room.

He clicked 'ok' on his smartphone and accepted the call. "Turn on CNN," said his boss' voice on the other end of the line.

"Hang on a minute; my other phone is ringing."

"Don't worry about it; that's me on that line too." As if to confirm he was telling the truth, the landline immediately stopped ringing.

Paul reached for the T.V. remote. "What's the problem? Is there an urgent midnight miracle that needs investigating somewhere in Rome?"

"It's not midnight."

Peter looked at the clock by his bed. It read 12:20. "My clock says…"

The Cardinal's voice cut him off. "It's not midnight in Miami."

The T.V. came on, and the CNN logo was showing at the bottom of the picture. A ticker tape, stating the image was live from Miami, ran across the bottom of the screen. For a minute, Paul couldn't make sense of what he was seeing. Letters were spinning in circles as two men took turns flicking them into the air. For several seconds the young priest assumed it was some clever special effect, but then he noticed another line of text in the CNN banner that read, "God leaves a message that he's going out for dinner".

The men stopped flicking the floating letters, and they slowly returned to recreate the original message.

"This is a joke, isn't it," said Paul.

"Yes, of course it is," said the Cardinal. "In fact, His Holiness The Pope is laughing so much he wants you on a jet to Miami in the next hour."

"You are kidding. He can't believe this is for real."

"Father Paul, you head the task-force we employ to investigate possible miracles and unexplained religious events, especially ones we deem threatening to The Catholic Church. What could be more concerning than God appearing?"

"But this is ridiculous. It's probably some hoax. Even if it isn't, how could this cause The Vatican problems? Wouldn't we welcome God appearing to mankind?"

"If God decides to talk to any random person in the street, where does that leave us? We work for God's Bishop. He owns the big phone to the man upstairs. If he gets cut out of the picture, we are all out of a job. Now, get packed and call me when you arrive in Miami. A Gulfstream is waiting for you at the airport, and you are its only passenger."

The line had immediately gone dead and, twenty minutes later, Paul was watching Rome disappear into the distance as the plane climbed into the night sky.

Now, fifteen hours later, he hadn't slept a wink. By the time the aircraft was on final approach to Miami International, all Paul could think about was the seriousness in The Cardinal's voice. In the five years that he had been running the Vatican's equivalent of the CIA, he had seen many unexplained events, but none of them ever alluded to God himself appearing to someone. Well, apart from the occasional person who was obviously certifiable. This was a different situation entirely, and it was made more complicated by Johnson's clear message that The Catholic Church had a horse in this race. The best result for everyone, especially himself, would be to find it was all an elaborate joke. That way, the status quo would be maintained. The Pope would remain the only person with God's direct number, all of their jobs within The Catholic Church would be safe, and Paul himself wouldn't be faced with a personal crisis of faith. This, by far, would be a win for everyone.

The wheels of the plane quietly touched down, and before they had reached the terminal, he had dialled The Cardinal's number to let him know he had arrived. "We have an address for you to check out," said Johnson. "It is the home of the man in the message. A car will be waiting for you outside the terminal, and a team has been assigned. Find out what's going on and report back as quickly as possible."

Paul clicked "end", and the phone went dead. He started to wish he had managed to get some sleep on the plane after all.

***

Mark slowly opened his eyes. The sun was streaming between the blinds in the large window of his apartment, illuminating most of the room. His head still felt a little fuzzy from the beers the previous evening. God could really drink.

GOD!

He jumped out of bed and searched for his phone. Eventually, he found it in the pocket of his jeans. As soon as the screen had unlocked, he stabbed at the photos app. A row of pictures filled the tiny screen. Initially, there were photos of his dog followed by a few taken at the studio and a couple of a glorious red sunset. He sat on the bed and thought back. If last night was a dream, it was really vivid. He noticed the slider bar on the right was not quite at the top. Using his index finger, he slid the pictures upward. A photo of a charming Hooters waitress appeared.

"Angela," he said. "Doesn't mean I had dinner with God, though. Maybe just…"

He stopped. Three more images had appeared. One was him and Angela, both holding what looked like tequila shots. Then another of the same scene but, sandwiched between them, God was holding a shot glass as well. In the last, Angela was missing, and it was just him with his arm around God's shoulder. They were both laughing.

After staring at the image for a minute, he grabbed his jeans and pulled them on. Mark tugged the door handle, and it swung wide. At the end of the apartment's long lounge, the sun silhouetted a small figure sitting on the balcony outside. He walked towards his guest, stepped through the door, and sat down next to God.

"Never stops surprising me. Sunrises just take your breath away, don't they?" said God, gesturing at the sun as it cleared the horizon. "By the way, I made you a coffee."

Mark picked up the mug on the table. "You made the coffee? Why did you make it? Couldn't you just snap your fingers, and it would appear?"

"I could, but where's the fun in that?" He turned and looked into the young man's face. "I have existed for billions of years, Mark. To me, your life lasts for the blink of an eye. If I don't take advantage of these small moments, it feels like nothing is important. The more time I spend on the simple things, the more I feel connected to the worlds I created."

"Do you get lonely?"

"Sometimes. But I have had lots of friends before and after."

"Before and after?"

"Yes, before this moment and after it. I'm timeless, so I have already met people from Earth's future. Well, the current one anyway."

"What do you mean the current one? We have more than one?"

"Every-time a change is made, a new future is created. That's why I try not to meddle too much. The world changes its path when I visit. Right now, the future I have already seen for you may not be there. I could have completely erased the future you should have had."

Mark rubbed his forehead, "We had far too much beer last night for me to process this right now."

"So let's just enjoy the sunrise," said God, and they both sipped their coffees without talking.

Below them, the parking lot in front of the apartment block began filling with television news vans.

"I wonder what's going on," said Mark.

"God knows," said God with a grin.

"So God, sorry Bill, what is really going on and why are they pointing cameras at us?"

"I left a message telling your team you were with me. I didn't want them to be worried."

Mark looked down at the view five floors below him. "You told them I was with God?"

"Yep. I guess they are here to see for themselves. Mark, could you do me a favour and bend your head down about six inches?"

Mark did as he was asked, and a bullet shattered the wall directly behind where his forehead had just been.

"Christ!" shouted Mark, diving for the floor. "Sorry, I didn't mean to…"

"I think we should go inside," said God as a dozen more bullets smashed the windows around them. "I think the moment has gone, and I want another coffee."

***

Jeremiah's house looked down on L.A. from the Hollywood hills. He had paid cash for it when a porn director hit hard times and needed to quickly liquidate his assets. Although the house had been used as a location in many X rated movies, it had seen far more debauched acts of sex since Jeremiah had taken ownership.

He could see Rebecca lounging by the pool in a red bikini. He watched her flawless skin shimmer as a thin layer of perspiration rested on top of her suntan lotion. On any other day, he would be lying with her, taking advantage of her nearly naked body. But not today. Big wheels were turning, and he had to keep focused.

In the ceiling, a small projector hummed quietly as it shone a continually changing set of images onto the opposite wall. The room looked like a compact movie theatre and the pictures covered about twenty horizontal feet of the white painted wall as well as the whole of its vertical height.

The cameraman was panning from an enthusiastic reporter to the balcony of an apartment block which was clearly lit by the morning sun.

The camera had an impressive zoom capability and cropped to a perfect view of two men sitting drinking coffee as they watched the sunrise. One was wearing a white soccer shirt, and the other was in blue jeans. Over the top of the images, the reporter was running a continuous commentary. "So, after the mysterious and unexplained note, supposedly left by God in an atheist T.V. presenter's office yesterday, we have traced the missing man to this apartment. His name is Mark Schneider, and we believe he is the bare-chested man on the right. This begs the question, is his fellow companion God? We will be broadcasting live from his apartment in Biscayne Bay and hopefully getting to the bottom of this mystery as the morning unfolds."

At that moment, the bare-chested man dipped his head forward, just as a shot rang out. Plaster exploded from the wall behind him. On the ground, people ran for cover, but the camera remained broadcasting from the tripod it was sitting on. More shots echoed from the building opposite, and all of the windows surrounding the little man shattered. Without blinking, the man slowly stood up, looked straight into the lens and mouthed the words, "nice try". He then picked up his coffee mug and walked inside, closely followed by the other man who crawled along the ground behind him.

Jeremiah stared at the screen. Had that really happened? It felt like the man in the white soccer shirt had been talking directly to him. How could he have known it was Jeremiah who had placed a hit on the atheist. It must be a coincidence. He had no connection to them and there was no way the little guy could have known he was watching them on T.V. at that exact moment.

When he first realised someone was pulling a stunt that could disrupt his money-making evangelist tour, Jeremiah knew he had to act quickly. If left unchecked, it could derail all his plans to grab the media headlines wherever he went.

Over the years, he had been forced to deal with competitors, nosy reporters and other conmen who had chosen religion as their career. Their disappearances and fatal accidents had never been traced back to his door. When he saw the news report with the clever message, he knew it was a setup. Something to gain publicity for a later con. Perhaps a new messiah or prophet. Whatever it was, it would damage his tour and cost him money. The last thing he wanted was the rubes to start sending his donations to an atheist who had miraculously been contacted by God and converted to the ways of the Lord.

Now things had gone from bad to worse. The hitman had missed. You would think the job title made it clear what his objective was.

"Hitman, my arse," he said. Jeremiah mused that life was unfair. If he sold ice-cream, it wouldn't make sense calling himself a plumber, but it seems contract killers are not tied to the same trade descriptions act.

He needed to take control of this personally.

"Rebecca," he shouted through the open window. "Get changed honey, we are going to Miami."

"Miami?"

"Yes, Miami. Big place, lots of gay people, salsa and giant cocktails. Apparently, it will be underwater in twenty years, so bring your wellingtons."

"Why are we going to Miami? We only just got back here?"

"We are going to see God."

"Does he live in Miami?"

"Yes, apparently he likes beachfront properties and the Cuban groove, now, get moving."

When they were first introduced, Rebecca had liked the fact that Jeremiah was a little bit crazy, but now she had the distinct feeling that the last wobbly wheel on the rickety waggon he carried his mind in had finally fallen off.

FOUR

"What the hell was that?" screamed Mark as he hid in the kitchen.

"I think someone was trying to shoot us," said God.

"Why? Why would someone want to shoot at us, Bill?"

"I am guessing they wanted us dead, Mark. If they were inviting us to a party, they would have left a note with RSVP on it instead."

Mark's head appeared from behind the fridge. "Bill, you are not taking this seriously. You might be immortal, but I'm not. Can I ask a serious question?"

"Sure, of course."

"Is there a heaven where I will spend eternity floating in a sea of bliss while chatting to Gandhi?"

God shrugged, "Maybe this isn't the time to get into the heaven thing right now." Two bullets blew holes in the door to the lounge, making it look like it had eyes.

"Bill, this is exactly the time to get into the heaven thing. I would really like to know if that is what comes next. Let me make it easy; if one of these shells rips a new entrance in my chest and an exit in my back, is this a good day or a bad day for me?"

"Put it this way, Mark, if I was you, I would keep my head down for another twenty seconds."

"Oh great. The bible is a bit iffy on facts, and now there is no Heaven. Would you like to pass on any other information that might be of use to me while we are talking."

"Yes," said God, "You need to feed your dog. She's hungry and very scared."

Mark twisted around and spotted Millie hiding under the table. He slid over and curled his body around her to stop any stray bullets turning her into a furry string vest.

Suddenly it went quiet.

God walked over and rested his hand on Mark's shoulder. "It's ok, you can come out now."

Slowly, he slid out from under the table and sat up. He held a miniature dachshund in his arms, hugging her tightly. "It's ok, Millie baby. All the fireworks have stopped." Although she was still shaking, she began to lick Mark's neck. He looked up. "Do you like dogs, Bill?"

"They are one of my best creations in this or any other universe."

"What are you going to do to the person shooting at us? Vengeance is Mine sayeth the Lord. Deuteronomy 32:35," said Mark comforting Millie.

"The Bible again?"

"Yep."

"Look, Mark, have you ever been misquoted in the media?"

"All the time."

"Annoying isn't it? You want me to kill the person shooting at us for trying to kill you?"

"Not me, but they shot at my dog." Millie had calmed down a little and was now licking God's hand as well.

He sat down on the floor next to Mark and began stroking the dog. "What is important is that you were prepared to give up your life to protect Millie. Now I know I picked the right person to talk to. And, by the way, I did say, "thou shalt not kill". How are you guys doing with that one?"

"Pretty bad, Bill."

"Sometimes Mark, it's better to lead by example than to dictate orders to others."

"You are a better person than me, Bill. I'd be a lot happier if I was kicking the shooter in the balls right now."

"I said you shouldn't kill; I never said you mustn't kick someone in the genitals who shot at your dog. In fact, pass me your dog for a second."

God took Millie, who immediately started licking his face.

"You ready?" he said. "You'll only have a second. You are looking for a bald guy dressed in a black T-shirt and carrying a holdall." God symbolically clicked his fingers and Mark instantly appeared in a hotel lobby across the street. Walking fast, and only five feet in front of him, was a tall man with a shaven head. The man was wearing a black V-neck T-shirt and carrying a canvas bag. As he stepped closer, he froze as his proposed target suddenly materialised out of thin air. Without missing a beat, Mark swung a size thirteen foot between the man's legs, who folded into a heap on the floor clutching his balls.

"God says Hi," Mark said and immediately disappeared as quickly as he arrived.

"Feel better now?" said God, playing with Millie on the floor.

"Much, now let's find some food for my little girl and then get out of here before the cops arrive. I don't think I could explain this without ending up wearing a straight jacket."

***

Father Paul had cleared customs and entered the arrivals terminal. Cardinal Johnson had told him he would be picked up by a car waiting outside, so he was a little surprised to see two men standing at the barrier holding a sign with the word Paul written on it in big black letters. For a second, he dismissed it as a coincidence, but then he noticed the "P" had been made to look like a cartoon stick man dragging a massive cross. Over its head was an oval suggesting the stick man was a saint. He had seen many similar images with halos, painted by old masters, while walking through The Vatican on the way to his office each day.

The smaller of the two men waved enthusiastically while the other struggled with a rucksack that looked alive and tried desperately to escape his grip. More confusing still was how they were dressed. Paul had used local security teams in many countries worldwide, and they all shared one habit, they wore black.

These two men were completely different from the norm and diverged from the standard dress code in his shadowy world. The tall one was wearing jeans, cowboy boots and a white cotton shirt. Paul looked down to the big man's side. It was the little guy that was the real problem. He was wearing similar jeans, but he sported an SS Lazio soccer shirt on his top half. Paul recognised it immediately because he regularly wore one similar when watching his favourite team in Rome.

Paul walked over and the tall guy shook his hand. "Hi Father, Bill has told me all about you. CIA for the Pope, how cool is that?"

Paul looked from one to the other. These people were not his support team. The smaller man stretched out his hand. "You like the shirt? I thought it would make you feel at home," he said.

As they touched, Paul's head began spinning and he lurched backwards, very nearly collapsing in the walkway. God held his arm until the younger man regained his balance. Paul's body was filled with equal measures of panic and calm. A large part of him wanted to run away, but the other never wanted to leave this man again.

"It's the temporal field," explained Mark in a way that sounded like it should make everything clear.

"Unfortunately, it affects people in different ways," said God. "Paul has a conflict starting deep inside that is causing him some issues, isn't that right Paul? Perhaps a coffee would be a good idea. I'm afraid it isn't as good as the ones you are used to in Rome, but it is hot and loaded with caffeine." He guided the priest towards a Starbucks, and, a few minutes later, the three of them were sitting around a table, each with a double espresso in front of them.

Paul looked at the tall man. "How do you know about the job I do? It is one of our best-kept secrets."

Mark was still struggling with his rucksack, which looked like it had a mind of its own. He opened the zip a little wider and a small dog's head popped out. Millie let out a little yap of happiness. "Shush baby," said the big guy. "You are not supposed to be in here; they don't allow dogs inside the terminal."

"I think I can help with that," said the small man in the Italian football shirt. He snapped his fingers just as a waitress walked up to the table with three glasses of water.

She looked at Millie and stared for a moment. "Nice plant," she said. "Mind if I smell the flowers?"

"Help yourself," said God. "It's an aspidistra,"

Paul looked at the dog sitting in the man's lap. "But it's a dog," he said.

The young woman leant forward and took a big sniff in Millie's ear. "Smells lovely to me," said the girl as she turned and walked away.

Paul felt his head start to spin again.

"Put some sugar in your coffee; the sweetness will help," said the little Lazio fan.

Mark leant forward and spoke in his best conspiratorial whisper. "Father Paul, you came here to investigate the message didn't you? It was about me. Bill left it," he said, pointing at the little man. "He's God."

Paul picked up a spoon, dug three big heaps of sugar out of the bowl and attempted to stir them into the tiny cup of coffee. Before speaking, he picked it up and drank the contents down in one gulp.

"So," he said, taking his time sizing up the older man. "You are God."

"Yes Paul, I'm God."

"So, why does he keep calling you Bill?"

Mark butted in. "It's less formal. Apparently, he's not the vengeful angry God of the old testament. Who knew?" He said, shrugging. "Bill sees himself as part of the proletariat. He's a 'feet in the trenches with the rest of the troops' type of god."

Paul scooped up three more spoons of sugar, dumped them into Marks cup and then drank his as well.

God leant forward. "Look, Paul, I know this is difficult for you. His Holiness has sent you on a mission. A mission that is only ever going to cause you problems, and I'm sorry for that. If there was another way to achieve our goals, I would take it, but, unfortunately, there isn't. Just remember that when you need to make the right choice, the answer will come forth. In the meantime, I need you to give a message to your boss.

Tell him there is no room in his life for politics and religion. It is time to choose. He has a chance to lead by example, but only for a short time. The clock is ticking, and religious organisations everywhere will soon have to change forever. Tell him it would be best if he was on the right side of history." God leant back in his seat.

"You want me to phone the Pope and tell him a man with a bag full of dog and a little Lazio fan claiming to be God is coming to get him?"

"We are not going after him, Paul, but when the 30% of the population who identify as Christian find out what The Catholic Church has been hiding for two thousand years, we will be the last of his problems."

"I need another coffee," said Paul. "Probably several."

"And we need to go," said God. "We have a busy day ahead. I'll get you another coffee before we leave."

"Hang on, how am I supposed to believe you are God?" said Paul.

Before the last syllable died, the two men and the dog had vanished. Paul jumped up in shock and knocked over a coffee cup sitting near the leg of his chair. As he looked around, more coffee cups started appearing. Within a minute, every table was covered with them, and so was the floor around him. In front, a small pyramid, built of little white china cups, was completely obscuring the wooden surface.

One of the staff leaned around its side. A cup of coffee magically appeared in his hand as he got closer to the priest. "What happened? he said. "What should I do?"

Paul flopped back in his seat. "Bring some more sugar, I guess. I don't think I will have enough for this lot."

***

Twenty minutes later, as Paul was still trying to pick his way through the sea of espresso cups that continually appeared around him, Jeremiah and Rebecca were walking down the steps of a private jet about two hundred metres away.

As they passed the steward at the bottom of the steps, Jeremiah paused next to him. "The Champagne wasn't chilled enough. Sort it out or get another job," he said.

Rebecca followed him about five feet back, struggling with a large case. She stopped and whispered in the steward's ear, "He is having a bad day. Ignore him; you were all great. Thank you for looking after us so well."

The man smiled and said, "You are welcome, miss." He looked at Jeremiah striding towards a large stretch limo. "If you don't mind me saying miss, your boyfriend is a real jerk. You should be careful around him." He walked back up the stairs as Rebecca watched Jeremiah climb into the car where he sat brooding, waiting for her to join him. After a second thinking about what the flight attendant had said, she followed Jeremiah and climbed into the car alongside him. "You didn't need to be rude to that man. He was doing a good job."

"Listen, missy, until a few days ago, you hadn't seen the inside of a private jet. God speaks through me, and you are lucky I have chosen you to be my companion. Maybe I will put in a good word for you with the big guy upstairs."

"With God?" said Rebecca.

"Yes. He may even notice an insignificant girl like you if he knows you are one of my congregation, but not if you keep sticking your nose in my business and offering your irrelevant points of view about how I run my operation."

Rebecca turned her head and looked out of the window. "Jerk," she thought but kept her 'irrelevant point of view' to herself.

Jeremiah pressed a small button on the console next to him and dropped the partition window between them and the driver. "Where's the burner?"

The driver looked in the mirror, "There are several of them in the storage compartment under your armrest."

Without saying thanks, the evangelist buzzed the window back up and opened the cubby hole. Inside were three phones, a pistol and two extra clips of ammunition. He picked up one phone and closed the lid, but not before Rebecca noticed the gun.

"Are T.V. evangelists in a high-risk occupation?" she asked.

He stopped fiddling with the phone for a second. "There are all sorts of crazies out there, Rebecca. Better to be safe than sorry." What Jeremiah didn't mention was there was always a chance of retribution from one of his competitors. It did not matter how careful he was. Eventually, a person would put the pieces together and realise the string of high profile preachers disappearing from the scene was very suspicious, and a yellow brick road of accusations could be paved straight to his door. The risk did not stop there. In addition to the missing and dead, several ministers had decided to take new careers. Each one was worried that a little black folder, containing videos and pictures of them in compromising situations, would find its way to local news channels. It was only a matter of time before he was challenged. Jeremiah had been at the top of the tree for over a year now, and no chancer was going to knock him off his branch. He dialled a mobile number and pressed the phone hard against his head to prevent Rebecca from hearing the other side of the conversation.

"What happened, Charlie?" said Jeremiah as the call was answered.

"I don't know, boss. I've never missed before. It was an easy hit but, just as I pulled the trigger, the big guy ducked like he knew the bullet was coming. Then I sprayed the little guy, and every shot missed like they were swerving around him."

"So you just screwed up?"

"No, it wasn't like that. I could have hit them with tennis balls at that distance."

"And yet you didn't."

"Boss, it was worse than that."

"How could it be worse than completely ballsing it up?"

Charlie hesitated for a second. "This is going to sound crazy, boss, but I was shooting from the hotel opposite, and when I escaped through the lobby, I met one of the targets near the door."

"Are you telling me you missed him twice?"

"Boss, he appeared out of thin air."

"What do you mean he appeared out of thin air?"

"Not there one minute, there the next. Like magic boss."

"Charlie, you are ex-special forces. Trained in martial arts. A honed weapon of mass destruction. So when he magically appeared, what particular means did you use to render him incapacitated?"

The line went silent for a few seconds. Then Charlie said, "I was a bit surprised, boss. I didn't have time to react."

"So you just walked past him and did nothing?"

"Not exactly. He kicked me in the balls, boss."

Jeremiah paused for several seconds. "And then what happened?"

"He said, 'God says Hi' and disappeared into thin air again."

Jeremiah hung up the phone and stared out of the side window.

"Problem?" said Rebecca.

"Yes," said Jeremiah. "It seems God fights dirty." He gazed into the distance and wondered whether he was dealing with a genius con man or hitman who spent the morning with his face in a bag of cocaine.

"It seems Rebecca, it is time to take the gloves off. No more Mr Nice Guy."

She was about to point out that he was not a nice guy the rest of the time before she decided it was another 'irrelevant point of view' that would get her into trouble.

FIVE

"What do you mean you met God?"

Paul had dialled the Cardinal as soon as he was in the car with the rest of the team. Four men in black trousers and jackets filled the remaining seats in the vehicle. All of them were holding small coffee cups. The man in front of him drank the last of his and placed it on the floor. As soon as he straightened up, another magically appeared in his hand. They looked at each other, then at the coffees. "Stop drinking, you idiots," said Paul. "How many times have I told you, they only reappear as soon as you put them down."

"What are you talking about?" said the Cardinal.

"Forget it, it's not important at the moment, what is important is that two men were waiting for me when I arrived and they took me for a coffee. They knew who I was and why I was there."

"Do we have a security leak?"

Father Paul thought about it for a second. "Cardinal, I think it may be a bit more complicated than that. One of the men was introduced to me as God."

"Did he look like God?"

"No, he looked like a short soccer fan. Lazio, in fact."

"Why would God support Lazio? Roma are much better."

"Because Lazio is my favourite team, God said he was just putting me at ease."

"By wearing a Lazio football kit?"

"No, just the shirt and a pair of jeans, 501's I think."

"Well that's good; if he was wearing shorts and socks, it would have made me think you were crazy. Why the Levis then?"

"Apparently he thinks of himself as a working man. You know, the proletariat."

"That's very modest of him. So what did this working God say to you?"

"He told me to tell the Pope, there was no place for politics in religion and that everything was going to change."

Johnson considered the words for a minute. "Did he do anything that gave you the impression he might be telling the truth?"

The driver finished his expresso and placed the cup on the centre console. As soon as his hand released it, another appeared in its place. It made him jump enough to spill some of the hot liquid in his lap. For a second, the car swerved across the highway. Everyone spilt their coffee, and, as soon as their cups emptied, another appeared in their hands, stacked on top of the first.

"Yes Cardinal, I believe there is some evidence he could be telling the truth."

Johnson ended the call with Father Paul and picked up the receiver from an old landline phone on his desk. It didn't have any buttons on it, but the line instantly connected as soon as he lifted it to his ear. "I need an audience with His Holiness. The worst-case scenario may be at hand."

As he put the phone back into the cradle, he noticed a small cup of coffee was sitting beside it.

***

"Why are we back at Hooters Bill?" Mark stood in the doorway. Somehow an orange and white baseball cap with the restaurant's logo had appeared on his head.

"We have to meet someone, and here is as good as anywhere. Besides, I'm hungry."

"Do you really need to eat?"

"No, but the human race really does make some great food, and I try to experience as much as I can while I'm here."

"What do you mean 'while you are here'? Are you going away again?"

"Do you know how big this universe is and how many worlds there are out there with life on them? I try not to interfere too much, but I do feel a responsibility. I did start the whole thing off, you know. So, now and again, I drop in and try to keep things on track."

"Have you seen what we have been up to since you sent your son down here to redeem us? This is not exactly on track. Wars, death, starvation."

"Could be worse. I really dropped the ball once before and let the dinosaurs get wiped out. They were just starting to show some promise. By the way, what do you mean, my son?"

Mark stared at Bill for nearly a minute. "Hang on, are you saying…"

"Look, Mark, you are going to have to get your head around some facts. I'm a straightforward person, aren't I?"

"So far, you seem ok. Certainly better than the Bible portrays you. You haven't flooded the planet or started to turn every one into pillars of salt. What's your opinion on slavery? If everything I read is true, you have questionable morals regarding that, genocide and women in general."

Bill frowned. "If everything you read is true. But it's not. Yes, I have talked to some people throughout your history, but every time I do, some mad new religion pops up and corrupts what I am trying to achieve. To be fair, I gave up for a long time."

"How long?"

"A few thousand years. In that time, you seem to have believed every nut-ball in a robe who has miraculously heard voices from Heaven telling him that the rest of you should follow them. I would really love to know what the deal is with The Mormons, for starters. Does it not seem strange that everyone who says they have spoken to me has conveniently been on their own? No witnesses? And no one has challenged it? Really? And as for women, they are the only thing that has stopped you from destroying yourselves years ago. And they can keep focused without blowing things out of proportion."

"So, Jesus?"

"Never spoke to him. Mary Magdalene, on the other hand, was a nice lady. She understood what I was trying to achieve. It was a shame the men shouted her down and decided to try and do it without her help. I think someone started some rather nasty rumours about her too."

"Ok, this is messing with my head now. Are you saying every religion on Earth was the result of misunderstandings and people playing politics?"

"Look around you, Mark, everyone who is in a position of power within major religions is actually running political institutions that control the majority of people on the planet. Yes, there are lots of kind and good-hearted people in them too, but the messages were corrupted so long ago, people think they are fact. So much so they are even willing to kill for some ideology which is as far away from what's morally right as you can get."

"Gay people?"

"What?" said God.

"Gay people. Do you really hate them?"

"Why would I hate gay people on mass? I am certain some of them are complete idiots, just like in every group on your planet, but there are far more who just want to be loved and love back. Evolution just took them in another direction. It's not their fault, so why would I hate them? Do you know where that comes from?"

"The Bible?"

"It's in The Bible now, but it shouldn't be. It all started off as a nasty hate campaign by a political appointee to a tinpot king about three thousand years ago. He started a campaign to malign a really nice guy who was also competing for office. All of a sudden, a local priest had been paid to have a vision that 'God hated gay men' and guess what, within a week, the poor man was stripped of his office and pushed out into the desert. A thousand years later, the story has been elaborated, and it ends up in The Bible, amongst other mistakes."

"I did think it wasn't in keeping with the 'God of love and kindness persona'," said Mark.

"Do you know what really bugs me? That some people think I would tell them it was ok to stone women and children to death if they disagreed with the men. Why would anyone want to believe in a god who thought so little of life?"

Angela walked over. "I'm surprised to see you two back here. We have had reporters in all morning asking after you."

God pulled the baseball hat down lower on his head. On the front, it said 'Relax' and below that, it had a tuna embroidered into the material. "Do you think we can get away with a bite to eat and a drink without being too conspicuous? We should be meeting someone here."

"I would suggest you sit at the bar. No one would look for God there. Who are you waiting for?"

"A slim grey-haired lady in her fifties."

"She is sitting at the far end already. I'll bring some beers over. Pabst ok?"

God smiled, and he and Mark made their way through the crowd. Outside on the deck, the manager was being interviewed by a tall blond lady holding a microphone.

"Who are we meeting?" said Mark. "Someone important?"

"You tell me," said God sitting down beside a very well presented lady in a two-piece trouser suit.

Mark stopped in his tracks. "Hi mom, I didn't realise you knew God."

"Mark, I've known God all my life. I did try to introduce you to him, but you decided to become an atheist instead. To be fair, though, it was only last week we bumped into each other at Denny's," she said as she smiled at Bill.

Mark looked down at him. "Is that all you do, graze your way around cheap restaurants?"

"Don't knock it; you can't beat Denny's coffee, and it is free refills all day every day," said Bill.

***

Charlie Denis was sitting in his hotel room loading shells into a large capacity machine-gun clip. He had a one-pound bag of frozen peas resting in his lap, easing the swelling of his aching genitals. The day had started badly when he missed his targets, even though they were sitting ducks. Then it had gotten significantly worse when one of them materialised in front of him and tried to score two extra points by kicking his balls over his head. Finally, it hit rock bottom when he had to explain the whole story to Jeremiah. He could hear the derision in his boss' voice. It was bad enough telling your employer you screwed up, but it was even more dangerous disappointing someone as volatile as Jeremiah. That could be life-threatening. He thought back over the last two years. Five people had been dealt with on the evangelist's behalf by himself and were secretly resting in unmarked graves. And they were just the ones he knew about. Somehow he had to redeem himself quickly before he ended up alongside them.

In the background, he had been watching a re-run of an old John Wayne western. It was on one of the local channels that split the movies into two parts separated by the news. Supposedly it was an excellent ploy to keep the ratings up on an otherwise forgettable local affairs roundup. Charlie glanced up just as it cut to a news report. A woman began interviewing the manager of a restaurant outlet in the bay area. "So, can you tell me exactly where God and his friend sat while they were having dinner?"

Charlie watched as the camera panned in the direction the manager was pointing. A very plain looking table swung into view. The hitman stopped loading the shells. Beyond the table, three people sat at the bar. Two men were drinking beer on either side of a graceful lady sipping a fruit cocktail of some sort. One of them turned sideways and started waving his arms in a very animated way. At that moment, he lifted his hat and used it to wave in the air before pulling it down on his head again.

Charlie picked up his phone and redialed the last number. "Boss, you are not going to believe this, but the targets are drinking beer in Hooters, and they look like they are meeting someone important." For a couple of seconds, the voice on the other end barked orders.

"Ok boss, I'll bring them to you."

SIX

"Oh come on, mom, how was I supposed to know God was real?" said Mark, throwing his arms in the air in exasperation. "Even Bill says The Bible isn't worth the paper it is written on."

"Please, can you stop calling God Bill? It smacks of disrespect." She turned towards God and said, "I'm so sorry, you would think he was dragged up in the gutter."

"Kids these days, Marion, no respect for their elders or themselves," said God.

Marion turned back to her son as God leaned around her shoulder, stifling a laugh.

"Exactly," she said. "You shouldn't give God nicknames."

"What? Mom, he is winding you up! He told me to call him Bill. Bill tell her!"

Marion turned back to God, who had adopted his best disappointed face and was shaking his head. "So sad," he said.

"Oh thanks, Bill, I'll never hear the last of this," said Mark with his face in his hand.

"And quite right too," said Marion. "Ever since you were a baby, I have tried to help you into God's good grace, but you were too clever and wanted to hang around with your atheist groupies."

"It's not my fault. If Bill hadn't decided to go walkabout for the last two thousand years, I might have believed you. A postcard would have given me hope he was real."

"To be fair, Marion, I could have made it easier for people to believe."

"Yes you could," she said, admonishing him. "And you could have done better with The Bible and all the other books of instruction. They have caused a lot of problems for innocent people."

God nodded. "And that is the reason I'm back. Out of all the universes I created, you are the ones who are doing the best."

"I would hate to see what the others are like if we are as good as it gets," said Mark.

"You are not 'as good as it gets'. Over the millennia, many other societies have found enlightenment and created beautiful worlds where every one of the inhabitants lives a fulfilled and happy life."

"So why are we special?"

"You're not, but you are a lot of fun when you are not killing each other. Lederhosen for instance. Brilliantly funny! And jokes. You are one of only three worlds to ever invent jokes. I have tried to tell jokes on every other planet where life has formed. They just don't get them. And Lederhosen. Do you know how few worlds develop bipedal intelligent lifeforms that look good in Lederhosen? None, that's how many."

"So, what are you going to do while you are around, sit here and drink beer with my son?" Marion folded her arms.

"Ha!" said Mark, "not so funny when she is having a go at you, is it, Bill?"

God finished his Pabst. "Marion, your son and I are going to get the people of the Earth back on track, or he will die trying."

"What? Why am I going to die?"

"Are you a timeless deity that can travel through space and bend the natural laws of the universe to your will?"

"No."

"Then I suggest you stick close and keep your head down."

God put a fifty dollar bill on the counter and pointed at Angela. He mouthed the words "a tip for you. Thanks".

She formed her fingers into a heart and said, "Love you" silently as she waved goodbye.

"Are you ok making your own way home, Marion?"

"Yes, my car is across the road."

God clicked his fingers, and he and Mark disappeared. She walked down the stairs and out onto the short turning circle below. Before she could step off the curb, a black van pulled up, and the door opened. Charlie popped his head out and dragged her inside. "You have a meeting with a very important person," he said as he secured her with a cable tie around her wrists.

"Is he as important as God?" she asked.

Charlie looked confused.

"I thought not," she said. "Whoever it is is about to have a very bad day."

Charlie ignored her and climbed into the driver's seat. He decided to look for a new occupation after he finished this job. Things were getting weirder by the second.

***

In Rome, the Vatican doors had been sealed to visitors all morning. Inside the private quarters, a small secure room was being guarded by two of the Swiss Guard.

Behind the soundproofed doors were twelve Cardinals, all in a state of panic.

"How do we know Father Paul is correct in his analysis," said a large man who was perspiring heavily under his robes. "After all, he is relatively young and inexperienced."

Cardinal Johnson stood up and paced towards the window. "Do you remember a few years ago when a new text was uncovered that told of a first-hand account of God giving direct instruction to Mary Magdalena in front of a crowd of people?"

"Yes," said the sweaty priest in a heavy Italian accent. "That could have destabilised many people's trust in The New Testaments account. Well, the person that tracked it down and secured it in the Vatican Vaults was Father Paul. He knows what he is talking about. If he says that God could well be walking the Earth, that's good enough for me. The question we should be asking is, what does he want after all this time away."

"Does Paul have any idea at all?"

"Not in detail, but it seems his intention is to disrupt our carefully balanced world in an attempt to bring down organised religions everywhere. It must be dealt with and soon, but we in the Catholic Church have to remain distanced from any potential blowback." Johnson thought for a moment. "Who do we know that would also benefit from this staying a secret and who also has access to international operatives?"

"Are we suggesting that we put out a contract on The Lord God?" said a huge man wearing an intricately embroidered robe.

"No, Signor Alfredo, I am just wondering if it is right for us to keep this important news to ourselves when other people of similar faiths may well feel it necessary to personally challenge his validity, in a particularly forceful manner."

Every face in the room turned towards the large illuminated map covering the far wall. All eyes fell on the Middle East.

Cardinal Johnson sat back in his chair. "Perhaps we can have some off the record conversations with our counterparts further south. I'm certain there is someone that can join the dots on their own if we supply the correct information. The Pontiff does not need to be informed of this. The less he knows, the better for him if things come unravelled."

SEVEN

Much further north, in Moscow's political quarter, the dots already had several lines drawn through them.

Alexi Lebedev had been woken during the early hours of the morning by a unique ringtone playing on his phone.

It was the sound of a very loud and irate, barking dog. He didn't need to look at the screen to know it showed the President's name, written in big red letters that were flashing in time to the dog's noise.

This was not going to be good. Alexi's sole purpose in life was to express the Russian leader's displeasure to specific members of the US government, depending on what particular bug had crawled up the government's arse that day.

He answered the phone. "Yes sir? The Americans have who? In Miami? You want me to express our concern that it contravenes our current arms treaties? Ok, so just to be clear, you want me to tell the US Ambassador we are raising our alert level because God seems to have chosen to side with the imperialistic forces of the USA against the great Russian people. We demand he is shared between the two nations with immediate effect? Yes sir, I will explain our position and stress your displeasure."

Alexi hung up, opened his bedside cabinet and lifted out a fifty-year-old bottle of brandy he kept for just such eventualities. He poured himself a hefty shot and stared at the glass for a second.

"Better safe than sorry," he said to himself and topped the glass up to the brim before dialling the direct number for the US Ambassador.

***

Rebecca looked radiant as she walked through the hotel lobby, searching for the designer stores. Jeremiah had taken a phone call and run out of the door, telling her to charge anything she liked to the room. She decided it would be appropriate to fine him for being a jerk to the plane's steward and treating her like a stupid girl.

As she approached the first glass window, she saw the dress displayed on its own in the centre of the vitrine. It took pride of place and shone with an incandescent glow under the mini spotlights. Above the waist, it had a halter neck and below, the skirt dropped in luxurious silk folds to just above the knee. The colour was the most wicked scarlet she had ever seen. Such a rich red that the owner should be arrested, simply for wearing it in public. The outfit was accessorised with a matching bag and shoes. Rebecca touched the corner of her mouth to make sure she wasn't drooling down her chin.

"Fabulous isn't it," said a voice next to her.

She looked to her right. A man in a pale blue soccer shirt, with a logo that seemed slightly Italian, was looking in the window at the dress.

"You would need the bag and shoes as well," said another voice to her left. It came from a tall, good looking man in jeans, cowboy boots and a white shirt. He reminded her of a young Robert Redford.

"Are you two undercover mall cops?" she asked. "Because if you are, you would be better following that group of teenage girls who are stuffing tops into their handbags." she nodded over to another store where three girls, who looked too rich to need to steal anything, were making a hash of shoplifting some designer T-shirts. As if on cue, two female cops stepped into the store and blocked their escape route.

"We're not cops," said the older man.

"He is God, I'm Mark, and this is Millie," said the other man holding a rucksack with a dachshund's head poking out.

Rebecca scratched the dog's head and Millie started licking her. "Hello Millie, are your friends part of the local care in the community program or just roaming fashion critics in search of the Short and Tall store?"

"I told you to stop introducing me as God; it invites sarcasm," said God.

Rebecca walked into the boutique and the two men followed her. A well-dressed lady in her mid-thirties met them mid store. "Good afternoon," she said, looking at God. "Are you shopping for yourself or your daughter?"

"I'm not his daughter," said Rebecca.

"Me neither," said Mark.

"Rebecca would like to try on the red dress in the window in size 4 and the shoes in a 7, please," said God.

"Rebecca would like to know how much it is first," said Rebecca talking in the third person, "and she would also like to know how you know her name." She rounded on the tall man.

"Mark would like us to stop talking in the third person," he said, "because it is messing with his head."

The assistant looked confused but walked back to the counter and checked the price list. "It's $9,000 and $14,000 with the bag and shoes."

God pushed Rebecca gently towards the fitting room. "It's ok," he said, "Jeremiah can afford it. He spent ten times that trying to kill us this morning." Rebecca snapped her head around. As she was about to defend the evangelist, something stopped her. "He's looking for you, you know that, don't you?" she said.

"Try the dress on Rebecca and, when you have bought it, you can charge three coffees to his account, and we'll tell you why we are here."

The assistant looked at Rebecca. "What size?"

Rebecca turned away from God so that she could address her directly. "A size 4 in the dress and 7 in the shoes."

***

Jeremiah's limousine pulled up in the parking lot at the back of the Walmart and parked next to a black van with dark smoked windows. Its side door slid open as he climbed out of the Cadillac, and as soon as he entered the van, the electric door closed behind him.

Sitting on a seat in front of him was Marion Schneider. Her wrists were tied with black plastic cables, and a large piece of Duck tape held her mouth closed.

Charlie sat in the driver's seat, twisted around so that he could see his boss and keep an eye on the old woman at the same time.

"Was the Duck tape really necessary? No one can hear her scream out here."

"She wasn't screaming, boss."

"Then why did you tape her mouth closed?"

"She kept nagging. 'You're driving in the wrong lane, you're driving too slowly, you should drive with your hazards on at this speed'. She was driving me crazy."

Marion rolled her eyes and turned her back to the driver's seat.

Charlie pointed at her. "See, she's doing it again."

Jeremiah leaned forward and peeled the tape off Marion's mouth.

"Miss Daisy would have told you to put your foot down," she said. "I could have died of old age if you had gone any slower."

"Killing people is never normally personal with me, lady, but in your case, I'm going to make an exception."

Jeremiah moved so that he was facing Marion. "No one is killing anyone just yet. That is unless I don't get the answers I want. Now, who are the men you met, and what scam are they running? I know it is something big, but I can't quite work out their angle yet."

"You are making a mistake. I was having a drink with my son."

"Your atheist son who leaves messages from God, conveniently where the media can find them. It's an obvious setup, a con. Build the media interest, get all the Christian punters out there excited by the prospect of the second coming and then suck their bank accounts dry as they try to buy their way into heaven."

"You don't get out much, do you," said Marion, crossing her legs away from him and picking imaginary lint off her knee.

"Listen, lady, I am not renowned for my patience. You don't seem to realise the predicament you are in. You are trapped in here with two dangerous people who wouldn't think twice about putting a bullet between your eyes, and you have no way of escape."

Marion disappeared in front of him.

Jeremiah fell back and tumbled over the passenger seat, ending upside down with his head in the footwell of the van.

"She's gone," he screamed. "She's gone!"

Charlie assumed Marion had jumped out through the side door. He pulled the handle next to him, climbed out, and his feet landed on the ground just as Mark appeared out of thin air. Without breaking stride, he kicked Charlie in the balls again. As the big man fell to his knees, Mark leaned close and said, "God says, don't shoot at my dog and never touch my mom again." Then he disappeared as quickly as he had appeared.

***

Arsalan had been driving for three hours. For the past two years, he had been working at the Kennedy Space Centre in the maintenance team, and his cover was now cast iron. During that time, he had managed to secure highly sensitive data concerning the fuelling systems on the new generation of orbital delivery systems, which were being developed as a matter of urgency. Within weeks, the big prize would be in his grasp. He was earmarked to take over the integration team, which meant he would have access to the complete schematic detailing the final elements that he was missing. As soon as that happened, he could catch the first flight to Europe and begin his onward journey home to the Middle East, and a hero's welcome by The Brothers.

So why, when they were so close to achieving their goal, was he pulled away on a fool's errand to follow a crackpot story in Miami? Someone must have broken their vow of abstinence and started drinking because that was the only way he could explain the message he received via the dark web when he logged in this morning.

"Go to Miami. Take field kit D. Trace target name, Mark Schneider and companion. Contact handler for further instructions when the target is acquired. Priority one."

Field kit D was a black ops kit. Four pounds of demolition explosives, two pistols, an assault riffle, a thousand rounds of ammunition, two timed detonators, a range calibrator and a suppressed snipper rifle.

He was being pulled off of a long term espionage assignment to assassinate someone? It just didn't make sense.

In the distance, the tall buildings of North Beach slowly came into view. He took the second exit and hoped God was with him and would guide him in his mission.

EIGHT

At that moment, God was trying to explain how he knew what Rebecca's shoe size was.

"Mark was telling the truth; I am God."

"Why would God waste his time shoe shopping in a hotel mall?"

"I am not here to shop for shoes; I am here to see you, Rebecca."

She put down her coffee cup. "Please stop saying that, and please stop disrespecting God's name. You may not be religious, but I am, and I take it very seriously."

"I know you do," said God. He leant forward and placed his hand on hers. "When your dad died, I know how much you needed to believe."

Rebecca recoiled from his touch, overwhelmed by the emotions, massive tears ran down her cheeks, and she stared open-mouthed at the small man across the table. "How..?" she said.

"It's something to do with a temporal..." Mark started, but God cut him off.

"Your dad was your world, I understand that, and to keep him alive in your heart, you clung on to your religion. On to what you thought was me."

Rebecca began sobbing and laughing at the same time, "It wasn't his time," she said. "He was ripped away from me. The man in the other vehicle had been drinking, and his truck ran a red light. My dad didn't stand a chance. His pickup was torn in half. He was stolen from me and the pillars of my world crashed down."

"He was a good man Rebecca, one of the best. He brought up a good daughter. I know it wasn't easy for him, but you were the centre of his world," said Bill.

Mark gently put his hand on her shoulder to try and comfort her. The feeling he experienced the previous day, just by touching God's hand, flooded his body. He hadn't noticed until then. Rebecca radiated warmth. When God had pointed her out as she was walking towards the shop, he had thought she was beautiful. But now, after touching her, the rest of the world appeared grey in comparison.

Rebecca turned her head towards his, mascara tracing small lines below her eyes. She leant forward and wrapped her arms around him, and held him tight. Her face was partially buried in his chest.

"So I will see him again. I knew I would. All I had to do was believe, and we would be together again one day."

Mark looked over the table with a deep furrow carved in his forehead, "Er Bill. Shouldn't you…"

She pushed backwards, breaking the hug. "Why does he keep calling you Bill? What's going on?"

"It doesn't matter what Mark calls me," said God.

Rebecca was getting upset. She glanced from one to the other. "Is this just a big lie? Are you two just doing this to get to Jeremiah? Using me. Using the memory of my dad, so that I trust you?"

"No," said God, "It's just heaven. It's not what you have been lead to believe by the Bible."

"What do you mean? If you are real, then heaven must be real. Unless you are lying about yourself."

"Look, Rebecca, I can explain about heaven later; the reason I am here is to warn you about Jeremiah. He is not what you think he is."

"Rebecca jumped to her feet. "I knew it. You are trying to use me. How dare you? How dare you use my family? Keep away from me!" She grabbed her bags and ran for the door.

Mark started running after her, but the door closed and locked in front of him.

"Let her go, Mark. You are needed elsewhere."

"But you said this guy is a monster, and she is in danger. Why didn't you tell her?"

"She won't listen right now. Anyway, your mom needs you."

"Why, what's happened?"

"The man that shot at us has kidnapped her."

Mark gave up trying to get through the door and turned around. "So what do we do?" he shouted, returning to the table.

God snapped his fingers and Marion appeared beside them.

"Mom, are you…"

God snapped his fingers again, and Mark disappeared.

"Where has he gone?" said Marion.

"He's delivering a message for me." said God, and he walked to the counter to order Marion a cup of tea.

***

"Father Paul?" the Cardinal's voice sounded urgent on the other end of the phone.

"Yes Cardinal Johnson."

"We want you to wait in Miami for a few days. No further contact with the two men is necessary at this stage."

"You mean God."

"We do not know if he is an elaborate fake at this point."

Paul put down his coffee and another appeared in its place. The desk in his hotel suite was covered in them.

"Honestly Cardinal, if he isn't the God, he is a god, or he has access to technology so advanced it seems like magic to human beings."

"Exactly," said Cardinal Johnson, taking a sip from an expresso that had suddenly appeared in his hand. "We need to be careful we do not add validity to his claims until we know what we are dealing with."

"Ok, but in the meantime, did his Holiness respond to the message I relayed from the gentleman claiming to be God?" asked Paul.

"He is considering it but believes this is a politically motivated move, designed to undermine the Church's global influence."

"But God was very specific. He said politics had no part in religion."

"Father Paul, we appreciate your concerns, but, as of now, you are to allow us to deal with this matter. I suggest you take advantage of a few days of relaxation while we see how the situation develops. Get some sun, take a boat ride, have a couple of Margaritas if you wish. I hear the city is famous for its cocktails. But, under no circumstances are you to go out looking for the targets again."

"Targets?" said Paul. "What do you mean, targets?"

The Cardinal's voice became stern. "Father Paul, phone room service, order a drink and relax. We will be in contact when we need you."

The line beeped as the Cardinal hung up.

As he put the phone on the table, he had a bad feeling creep down his neck. A couple of times before, he had been pulled off a case, only to find something terrible had happened to the subject a few days later.

Sitting on the desk, partially obscured by half-empty coffee cups, was a room service drinks menu. He picked it up.

On the cover was a giant fishbowl of a drink with an upturned bottle of Corona beer inserted into a green-tinted liquid. Underneath the photo were three words, followed by an exclamation mark.

"It's CoronaRita Time!" it said.

"You're not kidding," said Father Paul, rubbing his furrowed head. Then he realised he had put the coffee cup down and another had not appeared in its place. He picked it up again and put it down. Still, no new one took its place. "At last," he said.

A knock on the door of his suite made him jump.

He walked over and called "who is it?"

"Room service."

He looked through the eyepiece to see who was on the other side. The corridor looked empty.

Carefully he opened the door until it reached the maximum the security latch would allow.

The hallway was clear as far as he could see. Paul started to push the door closed but, just as it began to move, a small dog ran through the gap and jumped up at his leg. It was wagging its tail and yapping.

He looked back up and three faces were staring through the gap. The two men from the airport and an older lady. All three were sucking straws which were buried in colossal goldfish bowl-sized glasses with upturned beer bottles poking out of the top.

"Room service," said God, waving an extra drink he was carrying.

"I mustn't talk to you."

"Says who," said God.

"Says the Pope, I think. Well, my boss, the Cardinal, but I assume the Pope told him to tell me."

"So you do what your boss says?"

"Yes, of course."

"And he does what the Pope says?"

"Yes, of course."

"Good, so do you think the Pope should do what God says?"

Paul thought about it for a moment. "In theory, yes."

"So the Cardinal says you should have a couple of cocktails. I think you should have a couple of cocktails and, as the Pope works for me, he would say the same. Open the door Paul, we have a lot to talk about, and you will need one of these when I tell you what you need to do."

Paul thought about the logic trail. Johnson had said to have a drink. He wasn't going out looking for the targets. They had come to him. All fair, no foul. He unlatched the door and the three people walked past him and sat at chairs around his small dining table.

God looked at the cups covering every surface in the room. "Had enough coffee?" he said.

"Enough for a lifetime; I may never sleep again."

God clicked his fingers, and the cups disappeared.

"Do you have to click your fingers to make things happen?" said Paul.

"No, but a bit of theatre never hurt anyone."

Paul stuck out his hand towards the elegant lady accompanying the men. For a second, he expected a coffee to appear in it but, when nothing materialised, he shook hands. "My name is Paul," he said.

"I'm Mark's mom. Marion Schneider. Nice to meet you, Father Paul. So nice to see a young man follow a calling his parents would be proud of. I had always wished my son would join the church, but he decided to ignore his mother and become an atheist instead. You can see how well that worked out for him."

Mark slapped his palm against his face. "Oh come on, mom, not this again. When will you stop bringing it up? Ok, you were right, and I was wrong; now, please let it go for god's sake."

Marion rolled her eyes and started tutting.

Paul picked up the small dog and stood her on the table. She took a couple of licks out of the CoronaRita in front of him. He decided the dachshund was the smartest person in the room and started sucking the straw on the opposite side of the glass.

"Paul," said God.

Paul put his hand in the air like a traffic cop holding up a line of cars. God stopped talking and waited.

Paul and the dog kept at the drink until the glass was empty. Millie and the Father sat back satisfied. Paul waved as if beckoning cars forward. "Ok, go."

God started again, "What was their response to my message?"

"Why are you asking me? You seem to know everything that is going to happen."

"I know things when they are happening or have happened during my current timeline. For some reason, your boss's response seems to be vague. I can't quite work it out."

"I think they are still deciding what they should do. If I had to put money on it, I would say they are focused on maintaining the current status quo and hoping the problem will disappear."

"You mean me? What makes you say that?"

"They changed the way they describe you. At first, you were 'an unexplained event,' now you are 'targets'."

Mark looked at God, "Bill, this doesn't seem like a great turn of events. We started the day being shot at.

Now The Catholic Church are concerned by us. Is this part of your master plan?"

"Mark, my plan is continuously evolving. Contrary to popular belief, I am not omnipresent. When things change in real-time, it takes a while before I can see the impact of all the other variables in the universe. When we stood at the dawn of time, I set everything in motion. That didn't mean I knew how things would end up. It's the same with all the other universes."

"How many more have you created?"

"Not an infinite number but a lot. In retrospect, it would take much less looking after if I had stuck with just yours, but hindsight is always 20/20, isn't it."

"So what are we trying to achieve? Can you please let us in on the big plan?"

"Everything changes if you know what is coming. The more I tell you, the harder it is for me to make the changes needed."

"And what happens if things don't change the way you want?"

"You remember the story of Noah?"

"Yes, you sent a great flood to wipe out mankind because they displeased you."

"Well, that story is from a world in galaxy 2,756, and I didn't cause the flood; their apex race did. Killed 99% of all life on their planet. It's a shame really, they were one of the few three-legged humanoids that ever evolved."

"So what has that to do with us?"

"That flood was nothing compared to what you people are going to do to your planet if things don't change. In thirty years, everything is gone, and the surface of your little blue planet will look like a large pile of ash."

"So why not just snap your fingers and fix it," said Paul. The priest had quickly realised that his

CaronaRita instantly refilled as he took his last sip. He was now starting his third and had glazed eyes and a slight slur to his voice. On the table, Millie was asleep on her back with her tongue hanging out. "Why not just fix it for us?"

"Oh yes, let God fix everything you lot make a mess of," said God. "I have my work cut out anyway without having to clean up behind you. I will guide you, but the hard lifting has to be done by mankind. It's the only way you learn and grow as a race."

"So what do we do about the Cardinal?" said Paul.

"I don't know yet. I think this may be a two-drink problem." God started sucking his straw. As he did, he motioned for everyone to drink theirs. They all took several big gulps, following his lead.

Finally, he sat back. "There are a lot of people who want to find us, and maybe it's time we should be found. Perhaps it would speed things up a bit."

"So who else is looking for us?" said Mark.

"The US government for one."

"And how do you know that?" said Paul, talking with a slight slur in his voice.

"Because," said God, "I can hear them breathing the other side of your door."

At that moment, the frame exploded inward, and half a dozen heavily armed men burst into the room, waving guns.

Mark dived for Millie to protect her from harm, God stepped in front of Marion to shield her in case someone started firing, and Paul threw himself on his drink to make certain no one spilt it.

"Secret service, nobody move!"

The man at the head of the team walked over to God and pulled his arms behind his back. "Someone important wants to talk to you," he said, clicking cuffs around God's wrists.

Marion calmly stepped forward, raised her handbag and knocked the man to the ground. "No one handcuffs God when I'm around," she shouted.

Ten minutes later, she was bound and gagged for the second time that day as she and the rest of the group were fed into the back of four black SUV's.

Across the parking lot, directly outside the hotel's reception, Arsalan watched as the vehicles were loaded with the two men he had been sent to find. Into the other cars, the agents pushed an older lady with zip ties on her wrists and tape over her mouth. Into the next, a drunk man carrying a small dog and a giant cocktail was helped into the back seat.

"Targets acquired," he typed into his phone, "awaiting new orders."

NINE

Alexi picked up the phoned and dialled the President's private number. Before he heard the ring tone, a voice said, "Hello."

"Hello Mr President," he said, looking around his office, wondering where the hidden cameras were located. "I have news from Washington."

"Good, what is the news, Alexi?"

"The Americans assure us that it is an elaborate hoax, perpetrated by a member of the fake news in conjunction with an insignificant blogger on social media."

"Alexi, we are the fake news on social media. 60% of the stories shared are generated by us, and the remaining 40% that disagree with our rhetoric are targeted by our teams. We have even developed a new job role in the political services of Tactical Propaganda Troll. Now, what have the Americans actually admitted to?"

"The US ambassador has stated that God's choice of geographical residence was not influenced by them. God, if that is who he is, has already been given American citizenship through their fast track system and, as soon as they locate him, will be given a US passport."

"Alexi, the person who has represented himself as God, was picked up by an FBI snatch team twenty minutes ago. Please arrange for him to be given Russian citizenship immediately, and I want his passport in my hands in one hour. I will call the US president directly when I have it."

The phone went dead, and Alexi immediately dialled a new number. "Comrade, we are about to welcome a new member to the communist party. I need citizenship papers and a passport delivered to the President in 30 minutes and backdate it three months. Yes, the name? God. Stop sniggering and get it done." He hung up. The date would precede the Americans, therefore, laying a prior claim to the deity. He sat back in his chair, pleased with his clever move. "All we need now is an opportunity to talk to the man himself and explain the noble cause the communist party is fighting for," he said to himself and looked around the room one last time, trying to work out where the cameras were hidden.

***

Where are you taking us?" said Mark, trying to make himself comfortable in his handcuffs.

Agent Garcia looked over his shoulder at the men in the back seat. "You are going to be debriefed at a facility in the desert and, if you satisfy us of your credentials, we may move you to Langley, where a meeting with the President may be scheduled."

"How long will it take to be debriefed," Mark said, starting to laugh.

"Maybe two weeks."

"We don't have two weeks," said God.

"Apparently the President likes to take his time debriefing us," Mark exploded laughing.

God and Garcia looked at him and shook their heads as he rocked back and forth.

Garcia turned to God, "Why the rush," he said. "I thought you were timeless?"

"I am, but I can't keep whizzing backwards and forwards, changing things. It gets very messy. Can we just go and see the President now?"

"He's very busy. We have to follow protocol."

"He's having a bath," said God. "And are you trying to tell me you have a protocol for God manifesting himself?"

"We have protocols for everything," said Garcia. Then he thought about it for a moment and turned to face the older man. "How do you know he's having a bath?"

"I'm God."

"Oh yeah. Forgot for a second."

"I think we should just go and see him. It would make more sense than wasting weeks talking. We need to get moving." God disappeared. Garcia was looking straight at him as it happened. "What the..? Where did he go?" He said, looking at the younger man. Mark opened his mouth to speak but vanished before he could say a word. In the other cars, Marion, Paul and Millie disappeared, only leaving their restraints behind them.

Garcia picked up the radio. "Get a message to the White house. Four people and a dog may be trying to gain access to the President."

A thousand miles away, a phone linked to a secure system rang. The owner reached into his black suit jacket and pulled the mobile free. "Agent Miller."

"We have intel that says there may be an attempt to compromise the White House in order to gain access to POTUS. Please confirm he is secure."

"Please hold," said Miller, walking through the President's private apartment and arriving at the closed bathroom door. "Mr President, I have been asked to confirm your safety. Is everything ok?"

An irritated voice on the other side of the door shouted. "For Christ sake, can't I take a bath without you guys sitting on my lap? Yes, I'm fine, now leave me in peace."

"Thank your sir, I won't bother you again," said Miller, and he returned to his post outside the apartment.

President Jeffries leaned back in his bath. "Happy now?" he said, looking at the small group of people crowded around his tub. Sorry about taking your name in vain, by the way."

"Not my name," said God. "Nice guy, apparently, but Jesus wasn't me."

"But The Bible says…"

"Don't quote the Bible at him; Bill doesn't like it," said Mark.

"Bill?" said the President.

God stepped forward and sat on the edge of the bath. "Don't worry about it. It's not important," he said as Jeffries pushed bubbles across the water to cover his lower body. "Wow, you people are still hung up on that original sin stuff aren't you? Look, here's the deal," he said. "You want to know if I am a threat to your office and the country. I'm not. We are here to stop you and the other world leaders from killing every life-form on the planet. As long as you don't get in our way, everything will be fine. You will serve out your term and then go and play golf for the rest of your life. I really don't care about the appalling way you treat people, the crimes you have perpetrated and the dark thoughts swirling around in your twisted little mind. Sure, you won't leave with another billion in your back pocket. You already have enough money for several lifetimes. Your business interests and those of the multinationals who contribute millions so that you turn a blind eye when they exploit the remainder of Mankind, will suffer; but that's inconsequential in the grand scheme of things. If you get in my way, I will make certain your remaining time on Earth will make hell seem like a positive step up."

"You think that the entire population of Earth will welcome being told what to do by a God that has been an absentee landlord for thousands of years? I can destroy you with one well-worded Tweet," said Jeffries ,laying back in the foam covering the water. "Mankind has outgrown you, and the enemies you will make are too powerful for you to stop. If you think all religions will unite to worship you, you are more deluded than I thought. Who's to say you are the real God. For all we know, you could be the devil in disguise, trying to trick us in an attempt to give up our faith. A little conspiracy theory goes a long way on social media," He sat, smiling at his ability to cast a shadow of doubt on any person that became a risk to his power. It was number one in his political playlist and had helped him gain the office over more qualified and morally decent rivals.

God lifted his hand. In it was a small, yellow, rubber duck. It was dressed in a leather jacket and sunglasses that made it look like the original Terminator. "Please don't try to convince me you have faith and are a religious man. We both know why you needed the Christian vote. It's the only way you got into power," God tossed the duck towards Jeffries. "Best you sit here and play with your ducky while we save the world."

God disappeared. Marion stepped forward, picked up a toilet brush and then scrubbed the President's mouth. "Don't talk to God with that filthy orifice," she said and disappeared as well.

"Sorry," said Mark. "My mum is very protective of Bi…" but he was gone before he finished his sentence.

Paul sat on the toilet, sipping his Margarita.

Jeffries looked over. "So what's your story?"

Paul took another sip from his glass and stood up. "Nice duck," he said.

The President put it on the edge of the bath. Instantly another appeared in his had, this one dressed as a nun.

The father looked down. "Oh, that's not good."

Jeffries dropped it in the bath, and another appeared in his hand, this one dressed as the Queen.

Paul looked down as his glass magically refilled. "I thinks I goth the bether deal," he slurred just before he disappeared.

A tiny dachshund sat next to the toilet. Millie got up and ambled over to Jeffries' slippers. They were white and had the presidential seal embroidered into the material. She climbed on top and looked at Jeffries.

"Don't even think about it," he said, a second too late.

Millie bobbed down, peed inside and disappeared.

The President climbed out of the bath and started dressing. By the time he had his clothes on and made it to the Oval Office, three dozen ducks, all dressed differently, were scattered around the White House halls. He sat at his desk and reached for the phone, but another duck appeared in is hand, stopping him from picking it up. It looked like a tiny plastic Lenin, complete with a hammer and sickle on its back. He reached over with the other hand and pressed the intercom. "I want a direct call to the Russian President immediately."

A few minutes later, the phone rang, and he picked it up. "President Goncharov? I think we need to meet.

We have a shared problem, and it could cause us both issues. We need to work out how to deal with God."

Nine-thousand miles away, a rubber duck with red trousers and Mickey Mouse ears appeared in the Russian President's hand. "I agree; this is something our two nations should see as a joint objective." He dropped the duck and another materialised in its place, this time looking like Marilyn Monroe, complete with a white dress being blown into the air.

TEN

Arsalan was tailing the convoy of black SUV's carrying his targets when the shit went sideways. He liked that expression. It made him sound like he had been born in the USA.

He was thirty meters back, riding a black and green Kawasaki. Motorcycles were perfect when you needed to covertly follow someone. Fast, powerful and able to slip through the traffic.

In the distance, the leading SUV violently turned onto the side of the road, closely followed by the others.

"Shit's gone sideways," he said in his helmet as he closed on the vehicles.

Doors opened, agents jumped out and frantically started looking around the exterior of the cars. As he rolled past, he could see through the open doors. The targets had disappeared.

There was no point sticking around. Somehow they had escaped, and he was back to square one. This was not a good turn of events. He had already sent a message telling his contact he had found the men he was looking for. Now it would seem like a failure if he had to admit they had gotten away. Where next? Where could they have gone? Arsalan decided he wasn't going to figure this out quickly and, as he was starting to get hungry, he decided to stop to eat.

Ahead he could see a turning for South Beach. He took it and, at the end of the bridge, started working his way through the roads' grid layout. Eventually, he swung onto 11th street and spotted the diner in the distance. It looked like it had been there since the 50's. The sun reflected from the polished aluminium sides, and the windows shone with blue and red neon. Arsalan bumped the bike over the curb and parked around the side. As he walked up the steps, the interior slowly came into view. It was decorated in a period finish. Several stools sat at the counter, a few tables were positioned in the centre, and at either end was a round booth. Every seat had someone sitting on it. All except one. At the far end, way off to his left was one of the booths. Four people sat around the outside. Where the round table met the room, a single empty chair was sitting on its own. On the booth's first seat, a small man wearing a Manchester United football shirt was waving at him and pointing to the chair. It was one of his targets. Next to him was the other.

For a moment, Arsalan thought about pretending he hadn't seen them, turning around and walking straight back out. Then the little guy started shouting his name, and he realised it would be pointless to try and brazen it out. If he had already been made, he might as well find out who told them about him.

He walked over and sat down, making sure he could draw the pistol hidden in his jacket if he needed to. To his left, the taller of the two targets said, "Hi Arsalan, I'm Mark," he pointed to the people next to him. "This is my mother, Marion and another new friend of ours, Father Paul. He runs the Pope's CIA." Paul nodded as he sipped at his Margarita.

Arsalan looked to his right. The little man was petting a small dog that was sitting on his lap. "This is Millie," said God. He stopped scratching her neck and held out his hand to their new guest. Arsalan shook it as the little man finished, "and I'm God."

The room seemed to go into soft focus, and Arsalan's tense body relaxed. Then the words the little man had said hit home. He snatched his hand away. "You can't say that! It is blasphemy."

"Why?" said God.

"Because it is written!"

"Let me guess, another book that tells you what I said."

"Of course. It is wrong. You must…" Arsalan didn't finish. He looked down at his boots. They were covered in grey dust. As he shuffled them, more dust floated into the air and then, very slowly, drifted back down to the surface. The light reflected off each grain throwing strange shadows around him. As he looked towards the horizon, he saw a slight curvature, and beyond it, the Earth hanging in the black sky like a blue, white and green bowling ball.

"Pretty isn't it?" said God, standing beside him. "I think this part of the moon gives you the best view."

Arsalan stared at the part of the planet he called home. "How can this be?"

"You remember the God thing?" he placed a hand on the young man's arm. "Arsalan, that means lion, doesn't it?"

Arsalan turned away from the view of his home planet. "Yes, and in some cultures, King of the Jungle."

"It also means fearless, doesn't it? Why did your parents give you that name?"

"They wanted me to be strong and face life's challenges. My father said he wanted me to protect myself and the people around me. My mother was different. She told me to be a king, a man needed to understand the power of being vulnerable when required. 'When you are completely vulnerable,' she said, 'no one can harm you'."

"And which do you think you need right now, Arsalan?"

"I don't know," he said and looked down at the ground. "My life was not leading to this moment."

"Arsalan, all of your life was leading to this moment. Your parents knew it, and so do you." God let go of his arm.

Then they were back in the diner.

Arsalan looked down at his feet. A small outline of moon dust was surrounding his boots.

"We ordered you Steak and Eggs with a black coffee. Hope that's ok," said Marion. "We thought you would be hungry after the moon thing. Temporal portals give you the munchies."

As if on cue, a waiter placed a large plate in front of him and alongside a huge mug set off to one side. "You guys on vacation?" said the waiter, trying to bump his tip with a bit of chit chat.

"No," said God, "we are trying to save your planet, and my dusty friend here has been sent to assassinate us."

Arsalan's phone rang. In a daze, he lifted it up and clicked answer. A deep voice spoke calmly into his ear.

"Kill them," it said, "kill them both."

***

Jeremiah burst into the room and headed straight for the minibar, which was bigger than the average restaurant bar in this particular suite. He picked up the nearest bottle and read the label. In tiny letters at the bottom it read "80 proof". He dropped it onto the floor and picked up the next. It had a similar number on it. After five bottles, he found a Wild Turkey that read "101 proof".

"It'll do for a start," he said and drank it halfway down before he came up for air.

"Bad day?" Rebecca was sitting at the far end of the room in the shadows cast by half drawn curtains.

"You could say that. I'm positive it was weirder than yours."

Rebecca walked over, took the bottle out of his hand and filled a large tumbler to the brim. "I'll take that bet. You go first."

Jeremiah picked up another random bottle, grabbed the cork with his teeth and spat it across the room. "I have business issues."

"Really? Business issues?"

"Someone is trying to take over my position in the evangelical world and destroy the work I am doing. They are trying to scam people by pretending to be the second coming," he said, looking at Rebecca as she took a massive swig out of the glass. "I thought you didn't drink."

"God has driven me to drink, literally," she said, taking another gulp. "He came shopping with me for a new dress, and then I took him for a coffee."

Jeremiah sat on one of the bar stools. "Little guy wearing a football shirt?"

"Yes, and he had a friend with a dog."

"What did he want?"

"It wasn't a he, it was a she, and I don't think she wanted anything specific, although she seemed partial to a neck scratch."

"Not the dog, God."

"He said you are a bad person. Are you?"

"No, but I am a pissed off person. I talked to one of his accomplices today before she pulled some clever vanishing act. Whatever their angle is, they are good."

He walked over to her and held her shoulders. "I am going to need your help to stop them from destroying everything I have worked for, Rebecca. Can I rely on you?"

She slid her arms around his waist, rested her head on his chest and hugged him tightly. "I believe in what you are trying to do. You may be rude and an egotistical arse sometimes, but I believe we can do some good in the world. It's the reason I am here. I want to make a difference, and helping you reach more people who need the Lord in their lives makes sense. Tell me how I can help."

Above her head, Jeremiah smiled. They might see him coming a mile away, but Rebecca was so innocent she would be the perfect bait to get them to show their hand. "I need you to carry on just being you. They contacted you for a reason so they must think you are important to their plans. At some time, they will get in touch again and when they do, you will be able to play your part. This is what I want you to do…"

Jeremiah led her to the bedroom and explained his idea as the two slid between the sheets. He really liked Rebecca but, beyond that, he needed her to play a part in what he had planned. If she made it through the other side alive, it would be a pleasant bonus.

***

"Your Holiness," said Cardinal Johnson in his most obsequious voice, "I have made plans for Father Paul to remain in Miami for the next week. Although we need a local presence, it is better to distance ourselves at this stage. I believe the Americans describe it as creating plausible deniability. Our committee will manage our interactions with the person portraying himself as God. That allows you to avoid any unpleasant questions, at least for the moment."

On the other end of the phone, the Supreme Pontiff reeled off a series of comments and thoughts before asking the last question.

Cardinal Johnson evaluated the question and summed up the reality they were now dealing with.

"Your Holiness, some of our direct competitors in the secular world have also voiced their concerns and are currently carrying out an expeditionary assessment of the individuals we have identified. Based on the outcome, we will be able to decide exactly how to handle this, given Our Lord has decided to ignore the normal chain of command." Ten years as a US Marine Chaplain had left Johnson with many overlaps when it came to understanding the world around him.

"We have competitors that are now involved, and we believe it would be best to let them bear the burden of clarifying exactly what we are dealing with," he said, using political vagary to allow him to rewrite history at a later date if required. "You never know when you are being recorded in today's digital world," he thought.

It went quiet on the other end of the line for a few seconds but, eventually, Johnson heard what he had been waiting for. A commitment to stay out of the matter until Johnson told him it needed his personal attention.

"Yes your Holiness. I will let you know when the time is right."

He rotated in his chair and looked up at a large oil painting of God handing the tablets of stone to Moses. For a minute, he considered the importance of the scene. "If you two had got this right, we wouldn't be in this mess right now."

He slid his hand into his pocket and pulled out his mobile. After a short search and a press of a button, Johnson heard Father Paul's number ringing on the other end. When it answered, he did not wait for his operative to greet him. "Father Paul, I am containing the situation at this end, but I need you to keep surveillance on the man purporting to be God. At this point, we need to work in the shadows, at least until our hand is forced and his Holiness needs to become involved... ...Paul?"

"Father Paul cannot come to the phone right now because he is a little drunk and looking after my dog."

"Who is this? Why is a representative of the Catholic Church drunk?" asked Johnson.

"It's your fault. Well, yours and God's really. You have driven him to drink by placing him in a difficult situation he was not prepared for, and God, unfortunately, bestowed the gift of unlimited cocktails on him to calm him down," said Mark as he struggled to take the glass out of father Paul's hand. "Look," he said, "we are a bit busy here at the moment. Could you call back after lunch? Things may be quieter in the afternoon."

"I need to speak to Paul on a personal matter that doesn't involve you or the small man making wild claims."

"As I said, he is busy at the moment. We are having a bite to eat with God, and I'm afraid he takes preference at the moment." Mark was about to hang up when he had another thought. "It's Johnson, isn't it? Paul has told us all about you. Just a thought, Cardinal. If you turn to Proverbs 19:9, you may want to think about that before you call Father Paul again." He pressed end on the handset.

"What is Proverbs 19:9?" asked God.

"A false witness shall be punished, and a liar shall be caught," said Mark.

"Sounds like me, but I can't be certain," said God. "I think it got your point over, though." He turned back to the table and addressed the group. "My friends, as we are all together now. Perhaps it is time to formulate a plan to save the planet and move us one step closer to our goal. Between you four, I have the perfect team to take on the most powerful and dangerous people on the planet." God looked around the small booth they were sitting in. Mark was ignoring everything he said as he texted the office to say he would probably be late. Marion was posting a selfie of her and God, holding up a signed copy of her handbag-sized Bible, to her church's Facebook page. Arsalan had his head resting in his hands and was moaning quietly to himself while Father Paul was now unconscious and snoring loudly with Millie sitting on his lap. She was the only one paying any attention. God picked her up and scratched her behind her ear. She tipped her head on one side and started licking his hand.

God sighed. "Just the two of us then, girl. Maybe the monkeys were a bad idea, and I would have been better off with dogs evolving first."

He waved at the waiter and made a signing movement in the air to get the check.

"Never mind, Millie, we will just have to work with what we have got."

ELEVEN

Reykjavik airport is unusual in many ways, but the obvious one is that it has three runways. Even the largest airports around the world struggle to use such a vast capacity. Dubai and London Heathrow manage with just two, but Iceland's main airport has an extra one for use in summer to make it easier for approaches into the wind. The rest of the year, its shortest runway closes so that noise is reduced and safety is maximised.

Its length is less than a kilometre long and cannot accommodate the largest jets. Today, it only needed 10 meters to land the VIP plane which had arrived from the west. In fact, the aircraft on approach could easily land in the equivalent of four parking spaces in the short term car park. The F35 Lightning had cost $80,000,000 before it had been adapted to take a second seat. The one, now making a vertical landing at the end of the runway nearest to the aircraft hangars, came in at a cool $120,000,000. As soon as the wheels hit the tarmac, it began to roll forward and parked inside the nearest hangar in less than a minute. President Jeffries watched through the canopy as he rolled through the large doors. A white stencilled sign told him he was entering Hangar 18. "Ironic," he thought to himself as the jet came to a gentle stop next to a heavily armed MiG 35.

His own plane carried enough armament to start a decent sized war, and the Russian plane created a mirror image. If you stood back from the pair of jet fighters, you had the distinct impression this was a fight you didn't want to be part of.

As the canopy opened, the pilot stood up and helped Jeffries step onto the ladder which had been pushed alongside. "Do I have to give you a rating on Uber?" said The President as he let go of the young captain's arm. "Because that was the best damn five-star ride I have had in a government vehicle."

"Glad you enjoyed it, Mr President. I'll keep the meter running until you are ready to head back to Washington."

At the bottom of the steps, two agents dressed in black suits walked him to a Range Rover with darkened windows. Fifteen minutes later, they were pulling up at Dillon's Whiskey Bar in town. As he stepped out of the car, he pulled on a Chicago Cubs baseball cap and told his security detail to wait outside. Both men looked to their left and saw the twin of their car complete with matching security detail.

Jeffries walked inside and sat down at the bar next to a tall man wearing a blue version of his cap.

"How are the Cubbies doing this season?" said the man under the hat.

"Terrible. Lost their last two games and no sign of improvement. It's enough to drive a man to drink."

The man next to him pushed a bottle of Wild Turkey in front of Jeffries and then slid an empty glass next to it. Jeffries poured a large bourbon. "I forgot you are a fan of the USA and all of its decadent capitalist indulgences."

"My time in the KGB was spent in Chicago. When you wanted to blend in, it was important for you to drink bourbon and go to Wrigley Field. I caught the bug," said the Russian President.

Behind them, the door opened, and another man walked in. The two men turned to see who it was.

Goncharov turned back to his bourbon, took a big bite out of it and poured another. "Bog lubit troitsu," he said.

"My Russian is non-existent," said Jeffries. "What did you say?"

"I said, 'God loves the Trinity'. It means all things, good and bad, come in threes."

The new arrival sat next to them, picked up the bottle and drank five big gulps from the neck before he poured a large amount into an empty glass on the bar.

"It's good you could make it Cardinal," said Jeffries.

Johnson looked at the men's reflections in the mirror behind the bar. "We appreciate you including the Vatican in your meeting."

"As you are the experts in this area, we thought it was only sensible," said Goncharov. "But be clear, unlike the Catholic Church, we do not have seven Fridays in a week."

Jeffries looked at the Russian President with his eyebrows raised.

"He means that he believes life in the church is one long party," said Johnson. "And to be fair, we do enjoy our share of flexibility in our work-life. On the other hand, our personal life is more constricted than yours."

"Is that so, Cardinal?" said Jeffries. "The CIA seem to think that your social life, although covert, is very indulgent. Far more than your congregation could ever imagine."

The Cardinal took another sip of his drink. "My dear Jeffries, I think my small vices are overshadowed by the time you spend with your Press Secretary when you are travelling away from your family and our friend here who enjoys a continuous string of Personal Assistants. Let's not be concerned with the minor perks of our jobs. Instead, we should discuss the elephant in the room, our visitor who believes himself to be God."

"And what do you believe him to be?" asked Goncharov.

"We have an operative in Miami, Father Paul. He believes the individual may well be Our Lord come to visit us again."

"And where stands the Catholic Church on this?" said Jeffries. "Does The Pope recognise his claim?"

"The Pope is busy with many worldly problems, and we intend to keep him out of the loop until it is absolutely necessary."

"Plausible deniability," said Jeffries. "If you ever decide to leave The Vatican Cardinal, you could always apply for a job with our agency."

"Mr Jeffries, I prefer to stay in a position of power. You may control the lives of 300 million people, but we have influence over half of The Earth."

"So your operative, Father Paul, what does he believe God wants with the human race?" asked Goncharov.

"Father Paul is, at this moment, not contactable."

"I saw him," said Jeffries.

The Cardinal sat back, surprised. "Where?"

"Sitting on my toilet."

"What was Father Paul doing on your toilet?"

"Drinking a cocktail I think. He seemed a bit the worse for wear."

"Why were you in the bathroom with Paul?"

"I wasn't in there with Paul; he was in there with me while I was having a bath. So were his friends and the person claiming to be God."

"Why did God want to watch you take a bath?" asked the Russian.

"He wanted to threaten me."

"With a plague of locusts?" asked Johnson.

"With a plague of rubber ducks," said Jeffries, handing him a small yellow duck dressed as Elvis. As soon as it left his hand, another, dressed in Playboy bunny ears and a small white tail, appeared in its place.

The Cardinal stared at the toy in his hand. "So, God understands sarcasm? Who knew God was English?"

Goncharov took another swig from his glass. "The English make jokes of everything, mostly at the expense of those around them. Of course God is English. It makes perfect sense. Protesting he is loving and caring while he wiped out 99.9% of life on the planet with a flood. Only the English could square that circle."

Jeffries looked from side to side and considered the bookends he was trapped by. "You two need to get off your high horses. Put them back in the stable, and let's get working on a plan to deal with this situation. Earth is for Mankind. We don't need any random god telling our population what to do. That's our job, and we can manage quite well without anyone's help. Right now, we need to start damage limitation and lay a minefield in our population's minds. We need popular opinion to say that we do not want a great celestial dictator. I will Tweet that a liberal extremist, perhaps some extraterrestrial ethnic asylum seeker, who wants to sponge off Mankind's hard work and our Christian values, has made contact."

"And I can direct the news agencies to denounce an obvious attack on the communist party by someone secretly linked with the Western Alliance."

The Cardinal thought for a moment. "For us, it is easy, I think. We will give him the title of 'Devil's Advocate'.

Most Christians hate The Devil, but all of them detest a lawyer."

"Then we are agreed," said Jeffries. "From now on, we have declared war on God. He needs to know who is in charge. As soon as he gets the idea, we can negotiate a position for him that delivers our objectives and satisfies his need to be worshipped."

All three men clinked glasses and toasted their plan.

***

"Seriously, I do not need to be worshipped," said God, as he folded his arms and sat back in his chair facing the rest of the group who were lounging in what was left of Mark's apartment.

"So what's the point of being God?" said Father Paul as he popped a couple of headache tablets in his mouth. "Really, if you are not the big angry guy in the sky that we have grown up to fear for several millennia, what's the point?"

"I didn't choose this as an occupation, Paul. I was idling around after, I don't know how many billion years, and thought 'Let's spice things up a bit,'" said God, staring out of the window. "The next thing I know, I have created thousands of universes and suddenly need to juggle loads of evolutionary balls as you and the other disparate lifeforms, in countless different realities, suddenly start asking the same questions."

"What questions, Bill?" said Marion.

"Oh come on, Marion. You all have the same thoughts encoded in your DNA. Every life-form that becomes self-aware starts asking themselves the same things. Who created me? What is the point of my life? How do I make sense of the questions I can't answer about the universe? Each gap in your knowledge is filled by me. Can't make sense of the bad things happening, 'it must be God testing us'. Good things happen to me, 'I must be in Gods good grace'. How does the universe work? 'It's all down to God's wonderful plan'. Conscious lifeforms always reduce their answers to the lowest common denominator, me. Either I'm causing or fixing everything. I have to let you in on a secret. I don't have the time to deal with this level of detail, and, in all honesty, I don't really care. Millions of intelligent life forms have evolved and, after your tiny monkey race ends, millions more will follow you. Out of all the species in the universe, you are the most childish, the most stupid and the most endearing that have ever evolved. Think of it this way. Do you love the puppy who looks the most intelligent or happily gravitate towards the slightly dim puppy who jumps into your lap and looks at you with big eyes? Your race understands less about me but loves me more. And, partly because of that, I don't want you to kill yourselves off too early. In fact, I think you are the most fragile race mentally. The purest, dumbest, higher life-form I have ever created."

Mark leant forward. "Blessed are the meek Bill, for they will inherit the Earth. Mathew 5:5," he said. Marion placed her hand on her son's shoulder. "You are a good boy Mark."

"Oh, for my sake," said God, throwing his arms into the air. "You are not the meek. You are an angry, power-hungry bunch of chimps that were lucky enough to fall out of the right side of the evolutionary tree. I'm here to hand you a small chance to not kill yourselves and every other mammal on your little planet. If you disappear, I am left with the birds, and, trust me when I say this, there is no good bird joke that starts with 'An Emu walks into a bar, and the barman says why the long beak?' I like your jokes and your random acts of kindness, but you are all doomed at some time. You have too many flaws to survive. I would just like to help you avoid your obvious demise for the next few decades at least."

"Why can't you just fix it for us? I thought we were your chosen people," said Marion.

"I'm sorry, but the stories you have been told are not the truth. There is a lot of distortion. For instance, I told some of you that Mankind was my favourite; suddenly, that turns into 'Chosen Ones'. I have only visited your planet a handful of times in the last billion years. Mostly, for a well-earned break from the serious but dull species scattered around the cosmos. Think of yourselves as a vacation location for overworked deities.

Contrary to your books, I am not omnipresent. I do not read your minds all the time, and I'm not particularly interested in what you do in bed. That seems to be something your churches fixate on but, to be honest, billions of hairless monkeys swapping bodily fluids makes me feel a bit icky," said God.

"Oh, I feel so much happier now," said Paul sarcastically. "Mankind is just the comedy interval between other higher lifeforms evolving. We are the clown car that separates the trapeze act from the lion tamer."

"Don't talk to me about clowns; they give me the willies. Only humans could have designed the perfect alter ego for a psychopath. The emotionally destitute, the evil incarnate or the prehistory shadow in the dark. They all hide as clowns and jokers," said God, becoming serious for a moment. "You think the Devil will turn up wearing horns and a forked tail? No chance. He will wear a red nose and baggy pants. Seriously, you need to stop being so dramatic and think logically. What did you imagine? That mankind would live forever until the second coming? Look, everyone," the group stopped panicking for a second and stared at God. "Your race lives a single heartbeat in the life of this Universe. You are a sneeze in the handkerchief of the cosmos. If I wanted to be crude, I could describe you as a tiny guff in the underpants of creation. The only person that gives a rat's arse about humankind is me, and that's only because I have nothing to do before breakfast because that is where we are in the life of the universe. Its day has barely begun."

The group stood, staring at the small man for a long time.

"I feel very insignificant now," said Father Paul. The rest of the group looked dejected and sad.

"Guys, I'm sorry, but you need to stop thinking help will come from on high. You are a smart race and, when things are at their worst, your capacity for selflessness is heartbreakingly wonderful. If the rest of your people could stop trying to get ahead in this world by standing on the heads of the other sheep, you could do amazing things. Your lives would be easier, and your short time sharing Earth with each other could be more fulfilling. But stop thinking the universe even knows you are here. Greater civilisations have already grown, flourished and then died millions of years ago. And this is just one of many universes."

Mark stepped forward. "We know you are trying to help, but it takes time for us to come up to speed. You have to remember that we have used three books to guide us for thousands of years, and they tell us very clear stories, especially about us being the centre of God's focus. They say we are your chosen people and fill us full of ideas that may not be true. Take the Devil, for instance. Is he real? Does he hate Mankind?"

God looked down at the table in front of him. "Things got a bit much for me at one time. I needed help dealing with all the worlds evolving so quickly, that's why I introduced the Angel Core. They were supposed to help me delegate some of the more basic interventions required to keep everyone on track. It didn't quite work out the way I wanted. Have any of you worked with a disgruntled employee? Well, the Devil was mine. After we fell out over me choosing you monkeys to become the dominant race rather than cats, he left my employ."

"I can understand why you would choose us," said Mark. "The thought of eating dinner in a restaurant when other patrons saw no problem with sticking one leg in the air and licking their behind at the table makes me feel a bit sick. What happened then?"

"Then he went postal for a few thousand years until I finally had a sit down with him to straighten him out. Since then, he has spent his time dicking around with you guys. I didn't have the heart to squash him out of existence. To be fair to him, I was having a bad time as well and became a bit egotistical for a while. I can't blame him for losing the plot. No one likes a person that believes their own press, and I did for a while. In fact, I can say without hesitation, I was a complete jerk for a few thousand years. Anyway, he seems to be ok now. Occasionally he starts a war or releases a plague, but, most of the time, he is content with watching you people mess with each other. He believes you are the perfect soap opera. Hollywood couldn't write a believable plot where the characters do the things to each other that you guys do. Most audiences would think it completely unrealistic."

Arsalan put down his coffee mug. It clattered as it made contact with the table and attracted everyone's attention. "So it is the five of us against our political leaders, religious fanatics and most of the civilised world. How are we supposed to succeed in changing the course of humanity faced with those odds?"

"Six," said Mark, playing on the floor with an obviously hungover Millie.

"I apologise, six, including a five-inch high dachshund with a drinking problem," Arsalan corrected. "But even Millie's formidable abilities to sniff people's crotches and leave bare patches in lawns are no match for the entire American population.

"Why do you think the American nation, one of the most God-fearing countries on Earth, would be against us trying to save our planet?" asked Marion.

Arsalan lifted a tanned hand and pointed a finger towards the television on mute in the corner.

Across the bottom was a 'Breaking News' headline. Its red letters traced a repeating line under the news reporter's face. "President warns of a potential alien invasion as non-terrestrial insurgent disguised as God makes an appearance in Miami" it said.

"Turn it up," said Paul from the other side of the room. Mark grabbed the remote next to him and increased the volume, just as the picture cut to a clip filmed in the Oval Office.

President Jeffries' upper torso filled the screen, and he wore his best 'you need to take me serious' face.

"People of America. We are faced with the most serious threat to our nation since the attack on Pearl Harbour. Based on information from various security sources, the Earth may well be the target of a threat from beyond our world. At this stage, it is limited to a propaganda attack aimed at the very heart of our God-fearing nation. A figure we have designated X, a code relating to his extraterrestrial origin, has disguised himself as God. Using advanced technology to give the impression he has miraculous powers, he seeks to undermine our values, sovereignty, and, worse of all, our faith. This is a most despicable act, and I have given Homeland Security unlimited powers to protect our country from evil, unwanted, criminal aliens crossing our borders. At this moment, we believe the individual is here to spread panic and divide our nation. He specifically wants to highjack our great religious communities to use them in an effort to advance his nefarious agenda. I would ask that we stay vigilant and maintain faith that our Christian values will prevail against this most satanic threat to the United States of America. God (and I mean the real one) bless us all"

The picture cut back to the studio, where the image of the news anchor was surrounded by three other feeds from studios.

"For a response, we have asked leaders from church communities to give their thoughts." On two of the screens, religiously dressed men stared back at the cameras. The third picture was of a sharply dressed person with gleaming teeth and a thick quaff of hair. Jeremiah had the same 'take me seriously' look the President had worn a few minutes ago.

"Let us first go to the head of the largest evangelical movement in modern times. Jeremiah, what is your opinion on what the President has called 'the most serious threat to our nation since the attack on Pearl Harbour'?"

Jeremiah thought back to the years of media training he had bought. He leant forward in his seat, just enough to give the impression the camera had slowly zoomed in for a tight, emotionally charged shot that carried an important message. After a pause so long it would have made Obama cringe, the minister spoke with a deep, resonant tone. "Greg, the president is completely wrong." He let the words hang in the air for a few seconds before continuing. "This is not the worst attack since Pearl Harbour; this is the most evil attack on the peoples of Earth ever to have been perpetrated. Regardless of your religion, this sick attempt to usurp our great Lord's name deserves not only our condemnation, but direct action. The Bible, which provides us with his true words, tells us what to do. 'Thou shalt have no other gods before me' sayeth the Lord. He warns us against it specifically. The Bible even prophesied this moment. If we read Ephesians 6:10-18 we are told; 'Put on the armour of God, that you may be able to stand against the schemes of the Devil. For we do not wrestle against flesh and blood, but against the cosmic powers over this present darkness, against the forces of evil in heavenly places'. This X is from the heavens but not from Heaven. It is time for us to put on God's armour and, in the great country we call home to our religious beliefs, we not only have access to the best armour in the world but also to weapons that can be used in God's name."

Jeremiah's tone had gone from subdued to exalted in a matter of seconds. Now he was near fever pitch.

"We must take up arms because God himself tells us 'Blessed is the one who trusts in the LORD, those who turn aside from false gods.'"

Mark turned the volume down. "Oh good, now every pitchfork-wielding sky pilot in America is going to try to shove a three-pronged farm implement straight up my arse."

"It could be worse," said Arsalan.

"How the hell could it be bloody worse," shouted Mark.

Arsalan pointed back to the silent TV screen. It was filled with pictures from the middle east. Different scenes flashed by. Most of them involved large photos of Mark and God sitting drinking coffee on the balcony just before the shots had been fired earlier that day. They must have been stills lifted from local news feeds. The majority of the pictures were on fire, but some were also being repeatedly stabbed by a frenzied crowd. Finally, a picture froze on the screen in front of them. Two stuffed mannequins had the faces of God and Mark taped to their heads. Both of them were hanging by the neck in a mock lynching.

"Boy, Arsalan, your people are crazier than a tinfoil helmet," said Mark.

Arsalan pointed at the screen again, like the embodiment of the ghost of Christmas future. "Not my people," he said. "Yours."

Mark looked back to the screen. Under the picture, a caption read 'Montgomery, Alabama'.

He turned towards God. "I think the technical term is 'we're buggered.'"

TWELVE

At Miami International Airport, a short, olive-skinned man exited the arrivals terminal. As he stepped up to the curb, a yellow taxi pulled alongside and the driver got out. He handed the keys to the small man and picked up his luggage which bore tags with DXB stamped in large letters. Dubai had become a massive regional hub and was often the fastest route to get to the States from many gulf nations. The two men stood at the back of the car and one opened the trunk. The suitcases just fitted along the side of the massive black bag already tucked inside. "It's field pack D. Your targets will follow by encrypted text," said the driver. With that, he walked into the terminal and headed for the Tri-Rail train station.

The short guy looked behind him as a giant blond man, with shoulders that looked like a linebacker, exited the building through the same door he had just used. After a second glance, the small man climbed behind the wheel, slid the seat forward so he could reach the pedals and pulled into the traffic.

Behind him, another yellow cab pulled up to the curb, and the whole scene was repeated, except this time, the luggage tags were from St Petersburg.

The little man concentrated on the road as he drifted around the bend.

"Miami just became the most dangerous place on the planet," he mumbled to himself as a picture appeared on the burner phone beside him. It showed the inside of an American diner with a small group of people sitting at the table. He only recognised one face. "Arsalan, my old friend, you have made an enemy of the wrong God."

***

"Seriously, guys, we need to keep out of sight." Father Paul was pacing backwards and forwards across the living room floor. God had saved everyone an hour's work by instantly restoring the apartment to its pristine, pre hitman bachelor pad look so there was no shattered glass to dodge on the floor.
"No one would look for us here, not even my old boss at the Vatican. The operational procedure would be to leave the area and secure a safe house away from the action. We can remain here for a while until things die down a bit so that we can work out a plan and who to contact."
Next to the front door, Mark was leaning against the wall. "There is no one we can contact at the moment. In fact, I can't think of anyone on the planet that would be stupid enough to want to be within a hundred miles of us unless they have am immediate death wish. Anyone that dumb is the last person I want to see right now."
The knock on the door made him jump a foot in the air. Everyone looked at the source of the tapping, then at Mark.
He stared back. "I'm not answering it! It could be a mob of evangelical loonies with nooses at the ready."
God stepped out from behind Marion. "Mark, it's your apartment; open the door."

"Oh, it's easy for you to say, you won't end up dead like the rest of us mortals, and as I said, there is no one on the planet I want to see on the other side of that door."

A small female voice on the other side said, "Well if that's how you feel, I'll go."

Mark immediately flushed red, panicked and grabbed at the handle. As it swung wide, Rebecca, dressed in the scarlet dress from the mall, slid through the gap and into his arms.

"I didn't know where else to go," she sobbed. Her makeup had streaked black rivers below her bloodshot eyes. Even to herself, her act was convincing, but she was not ready for how it felt when the young man held her close. She had never felt so safe. Emotion overwhelmed her just as it had when she had touched the man pretending to be God. All the strength went out of her legs, and Mark caught her before she hit the ground. She was so light he easily lifted her into the air and laid her on the sofa.

"What did Jeremiah do to you?" asked Mark, as the rest of the group crowded around her.

"Here goes," she thought. "This is my shot at an Oscar."

She held Mark's hand tight and forced herself to look him in the eyes. "Before he left for his T.V. interview, he was raging about you both. Saying terrible things. Threatening all manner of violence. I tried to calm him down, but he accused me of betraying him and siding with you. He became physical and threw me out."

Inside his body, Mark could feel his blood start to boil. There was something that made him feel very protective whenever Rebecca was close. "This guy has just gone right to the top of my list."

"What list?" said Marion.

"My' first to get punched in the face when I meet them' list," said Mark.

Marion frowned. "You have a list for that? Who else is on it?"

Mark looked up at his mom. "Most people have a list, mom. It allows us to manage the anger we feel towards morons that inflict pain and injustice on us."

"That's not very Christian, Mark; who else is on your list?" his mother had adopted her best schoolmarm voice.

Her son thought for a moment. "The guy who appeared in the Times when he spent thirty grand to fly to Africa and kill a lion. Obviously, Harvey Weinstein, but I think I am way down the queue with many women in front of me ready to punch him."

"Anyone else?" said Marion.

"Oh yes, I nearly forgot, the man that invented the bagpipes, but I guess he's already dead."

"It's not normal. Mark, no-one else has an angry, 'punch him in the face' list," said his mother.

"Actually, I do," said Arsalan.

"Me too," Father Paul admitted, hanging his head in shame as Marion tutted at him.

She was about to turn back to her son when she realised God had stepped behind a large potted plant in the middle of the room, which had suddenly appeared out of thin air. "Not you too?" she said, leaning around its side.

"It's the bagpipe guy," said God. He's on my list too. Not that I would actually punch him, but I have thought about it a couple of times."

Marion sat down beside Rebecca. "How about you, young lady? Do you have an angry list too?"

Rebecca thought for a moment. She was surprised to realise she didn't. "No, I don't," she said. "Some people upset me occasionally, but I normally feel sorry for them. I guess something unfortunate has happened to them to provoke their bad behaviour."

Mark's mother smiled. "My name is Marion. You are a saint sweetheart and the only godly person in this room." Marion shot a sideways glance at Bill, who didn't notice. He was too busy watching Rebecca. His face was a mixture of satisfaction and disappointment.

"Yes," he said to himself, turning towards the kitchen to pour another coffee. "Godly indeed."

Several storeys below them, a white van with a big fairy on the side pulled up to the main doors. It advertised Tinkerbells' Cleaning Services. In reception, the security guard read the slogan on the back as it reversed towards the building. "Our cleaning fairies magic dirt away in a flash".

As it approached the curb, the engine revved slightly, and the rear wheels bumped onto the sidewalk. Because the entrance was recessed into the building, the van was halfway inside when it stopped three feet from the doors.

The security guard met it as the engine died. "Hey man, you can't park here," he said as he approached the opening door. The whole van tipped sideways as a giant of a man climbed out. As soon as his weight was on the ground, the van levelled out again. Before the guard could open his mouth, a huge hand grabbed him, pinned his palms behind his back and clicked a pair of handcuffs in place around his wrists. Suddenly the side door was slid back, and he was thrown inside. A lock clicked in place behind him.

"Hey, what's going on?" he shouted at the top of his voice as he lay face down on the floor of the van. Outside he heard footsteps running away, and another engine start up and roar away. As he looked up, he realised he was surrounded by large gasoline drums. Four inches in front of his face was a red digital readout connected to five blocks about the size of cigarette cartons. He had seen them before when he was in the military. They were made of C4. He looked back at the display. It said "3", then "2", and as the figure turned to "1", he started praying.

***

Alexi Lebedev sat next to his boss in a large situation room housed just off of Red Square. On the giant screen in front of them, a satellite image looked down on a white apartment block next to the blue waters of Brickell Key. A short four-lane bridge joined it to Miami's city centre. At the far end of the bridge, a white van started crossing onto the tiny island.

"Are we certain this will not trigger a full-blown international incident, Mr President? This will be the first Russian bomb set off on American soil since the Cold War."

"Alexi, you worry too much."

"But if the CIA trace the van and the explosives, they may follow the trail of breadcrumbs back to our door, Mr Goncharov." Alexi wished he had brought his bottle of Cognac with him. It may not have eased his conscience, but it would have anaesthetised it.

Goncharov placed his hand on Lebedev's shoulder and leaned close in a conspiratorial manner. "Don't worry about the CIA; where do you think the van came from?"

Alexi swivelled his head to check if his boss was joking. No smile, no sarcastic smirk, just a raised eyebrow before he turned back to the screen.

The van was backing towards the building. Whichever satellite had been repurposed for this operation provided an extraordinary resolution. The men could even see the vehicle rock slightly as a huge man stepped out through its door. Another man met him on the sidewalk and, in a matter of seconds, he was grabbed and thrown into the van.

The big guy started running back to the road, where he jumped onto a motorcycle are accelerated away. Seconds later, the picture turned white, and all of its fine details vanished. When the image eventually stabilised, the van was gone, and so was one side of the building. What remained was on fire. It was an inferno. Glass from the building opposite covered the street and masonry was scattered for a hundred yards.

President Goncharov leant forward and opened a small draw in his desk. He reached in and lifted out a decanter and two glasses. Alexi had heard about a Louis XIII Black Pearl cognac decanter, but at €16,000 a bottle, it was even out of his price range for a daily tipple.

Goncharov poured two measures, each of which was large enough to pickle a chubby guinea pig. "Alexi, I think we may have a reason to celebrate."

Lebedev took the drink and chugged half of it down.

"You should savour it, my friend. This is something to sip slowly," said the President, as he offered to refill the smaller man's glass. Before Goncharov could pour any more, Alexi let the crystal slip out of his hand, and it shattered on the stone floor.

"Christ Lebedev, be careful. This costs more than gold. Alexi...?"

The Russian head of state followed the other man's fixed stare. On the screen, standing on what was left of the top balcony, covered in concrete dust and flicking the bird towards the satellite's camera, was a small, angry man holding a limp dog's body in his arms.

Goncharov lifted the decanter to his lips, started drinking and didn't stop until it was empty.

***

A gentle knock echoed through the ancient oak doors of Cardinal Johnson's bedroom suite. "May I bring your morning coffee, Your Eminence?"

The old man sat up and leant against the massive carved headboard. "Yes Pierre, you may."

The door opened and a frail, grey-haired man dressed in black entered with a tray. He was so skinny, Johnson believed a sharp breeze could snap him in two. From a distance, he looked like a giant pip-pet filled with Guinness.

"Do you have a busy day planned, Cardinal Johnson?"

The priest switched on the television. "I do not believe so Piere, I am waiting for information from America before I can start my work. It may be days before anything happens."

He lifted the coffee cup to his lips, took a sip and then spat it across the room. Johnson began coughing so badly Pierre began slapping his back as hard as he could, which was not hard at all. A mouse wearing fluffy slippers would have made more of an impact.

"Your Eminence, are you ok?"

Slowly the Cardinal recovered and stared at the T.V. "Contact the airport; I want to leave for the USA in thirty minutes." Johnson climbed out of bed and headed for the shower. Behind him, Pierre began wiping coffee off of the floor. As he straightened up, he noticed some drops on the screen attached to the wall. Lifting his cloth, he began cleaning its surface. Just as he finished, he saw a face he recognised. Someone from the Vatican. Paul, he thought, his name was Paul. He had served him drinks in the presence of the Cardinal before.

Father Paul, that was his name. But why was a Catholic Priest from the Holy City being carried out of a burning tower block on American television?

THIRTEEN

Arsalan's head was ringing. He had never taken a drop of alcohol in his life, but friends of his had described their hangovers after wild nights out. One, in particular, had told him it felt like his head was banging inside a giant bell while a thousand tiny trumpeters accompanied the clanging from inside his skull.

"Close," thought the young man, "but you need to add a couple of dozen drummers to get to this level." He turned on his side and tried to open his eyes. As soon as he did, the white walls and bright lights made him close them again. With what little he saw, it was obvious he was in the hospital. The sound of a door opening behind him was just audible over the ringing in his ears.

Someone sat in the chair by his bed. After a few minutes, a familiar voice pierced the din in his head.

"What were you thinking, Arsalan?"

"As-Salam Alaikum, how are you Aayan?"

"Troubled, my old friend, very troubled. I have been sent to kill you and this a not a deed that brings me honour." The small man sat patiently, waiting for the young man to sit up. Eventually, Arsalan quieted the marching band between his ears and pulled himself upright. Muscles throughout his shoulder screamed with pain, and he guessed it would be a million times worse when the inevitable drugs he must have been given wore off.

"I am confused Aayan, why are we having this conversation? The smart thing would be for you to have killed me in my sleep."

"Yes it would, but I think your conversation would have been less interesting if you were not breathing."

"So what would you like to talk about, my friend?" Arsalan leant forward to relieve the pressure on his damaged shoulder.

A gun appeared in the small man's hand as if it had materialised out of thin air. A small suppressor was attached to the noisy end, which, in turn, was pointed at Arsalan's head.

He slowly leant back in the bed. "It's ok Aayan, I offer you no threat. Now, where were we?"

"You were about to tell me why you are following this false God."

"As opposed to your false Caliphs?"

The gun lifted in the air. "Be careful, friend, if you blaspheme again, you will leave me no choice."

"I do not blaspheme; I tell you the truth. This is Allah. Maybe not as he has been described to us, but he is the one that created the universe. I have seen the truth. He is God."

"You have been fooled, Arsalan, and because of that, I will allow you a day to come to your senses and rejoin us. Call it the payment of an old debt."

Five years earlier, in a far, far different world than the one they now lived in, the young man had managed to save his friend's life by cleverly getting himself in the firing line of a bullet meant for Aayan. Although it was luck, his friend always felt indebted to him.

"You may as well kill me now; I will not change my mind."

"I still give you a day. For old times sake. In the meantime, I must finish the job you were sent here to do."

Arsalan leapt forward but met the barrel of the gun travelling in the opposite direction. He fell back against the bed, unconscious and with a couple of additional orchestras playing in his head.

Aayan slid the pistol into his jacket and opened the door, 'ila-liqaa' my friend, until tomorrow," and he let it close quietly behind him.

***

"Mr President, our intel leads us to believe the Russians were behind the bombing in Miami.

We have to take control of the investigation. It is the jurisdiction of Homeland Security or, if not, the FBI."

Harry Jacobs had survived three consecutive presidential administrations and firmly expected to make it through a fourth.

"Harry, let it go. I have told you. The CIA have feet on the ground and will take point on this investigation."

"But..."

"Harry, the CIA have this one, exclusively. End of. Anyway, your teams are going to be very busy with another maximum-security operation." Jeffries pushed a thin vanilla folder across the table.

Jacobs opened it and read the first few lines. "You have to be kidding, sir?"

"What's brown and sticky, Harry?"

"Mr President?" Jacobs was confused.

"What is brown and sticky?"

"I am sorry, sir, I have no idea."

"You don't have any pre-school kids, do you? It's a stick, Harry. A stick is brown and sticky. You see, that is me when I'm joking. Now, this is me when I'm not. Take the file, make arrangements and don't screw it up. Unless, of course, you want to be franking letters in the basement of a derelict government office in Alaska until you retire."

"Are we certain this is a good idea, given what has just happened in Miami?"

President Jeffries folded his arms. "Do you know what this desk is called, Harry?"

Jacobs looked down at the massive piece of furniture taking up centre stage in the Oval Office.

"It has a name, sir?"

Yes, Harry, it is called The Resolute Desk. Resolute, because the decisions made here are cast in stone. It is resolute and so am I. Take the file and make the arrangements."

"Yes sir."

It took fifteen minutes for Jacobs to get back to his office on Virginia Avenue. As soon as he arrived, he called his two assistants and instructed them to follow him into his office.

"Gentlemen, we have to prepare for a visitor. Mr Goncharov, the Russian President, will be wheels-down in four hours at Langley; let's try not to let him get killed on U.S. soil."

***

"Explain it to me again, boss."

Jeremiah rested his head on the bar in front of him. "We need to find out where Rebecca was taken after the explosion. How many ways do I have to tell you,

Charlie? I need to find out what these people's plans are and the only one who can tell me is Rebecca."
Jeremiah paced the length of the bar in his room, picking up randomly scattered glasses of Bourbon like a marathon runner taking on liquid as he passed. As he lifted each one to his mouth, he drained it, dropped the glass to the floor and moved on.
"So I'll call the local hospitals boss. No problem."
"She's not in one, I checked. Nor with the police. I even checked with the coroner. She has vanished."
"She can't have vanished; someone must know where she is, Jeremiah."
"Well, if they do Charlie, I wish we could find them because, up to now, I have offered a $20,000 reward for information that helps us find her. Let's go. Maybe if we speak to the media, they will help."
Jeremiah opened the door as a young man, dressed in a waiter's outfit, was about to knock on the other side.
"Mr Jeremiah?" he said, as he stopped just shy of rapping on the evangelist's forehead.
"Yes, what do you want?"
"You offered $20,000 for information that leads to finding the whereabouts of your friend Rebecca?"
"Yes, do you have information?"
"Do you have cash, sir?"
Jeremiah waited for a few seconds. The young man looked well presented, but the suit had been cleaned a thousand times. $20,000 was a very serious number to this guy, and Jeremiah knew half that would be enough to squeeze all he needed out of the waiter. The evangelist slid his hand into his jacket. "I have $5,000 now; where is she?"
The impoverished waiter looked at the pile of bills and tried not to have a premature physical response to its sexy texture.

"$10,000, now, $10,000 later, and I will take you to her."

On his last trip to Asia, Jeremiah had bought a small hotel, two horses and the female contingent of a local family for what this man was asking. He balanced the deal in his head. Was Rebecca worth an eight-room building, a brace of ponies and a mother with three mid-teens daughters?

Given the circumstances, the balance tipped in the waiter's favour.

"$10,000, and you make certain I am adequately entertained while I am here." Jeremiah reached into his other pocket and pulled out a small roll of $1000 notes. He peeled five off and added them to the other pile of cash in his hand. The dishevelled waiter caressed it in a way that suggested he would sleep with the notes spread on his bed tonight. He stuffed the roll into his jacket and reached to the right-hand side of the door, and pulled Rebecca into view. She was stoned, definitely dazed by pain killers but semiconscious. Her dress hung in tatters. Part of her right thigh dripped with blood, and a deep cut crossed her collar bone.

"Christ," Jeremiah shouted. "What the hell happened to her?"

"I think she was blown up, Mr Jeremiah. I found her in the basement; I guess she was trying to get back to you."

"Thank you for your kind help and Christian values," said the preacher. "Now piss off before I ask my friend to kill you." Charlie swung into view, and the waiter didn't stick around to find out if Jeremiah was serious.

As the door closed, the evangelist pushed Rebecca into Charlie's arms and ran for the first aid cabinet. "Lay her on the sofa, Charlie." Then he stopped in his tracks. "Actually, lay her on the bed. If she bleeds on the furniture, I will lose my deposit. It's easier to wash sheets."

Charlie stopped for a moment and looked down at the beautiful, limp girl in his arms. "What the hell was she doing with this arsehole?" he thought. Then he shook himself out of it and carried her to the master suite. As soon as he laid her down, Jeremiah arrived with what looked like a triage kit. He pulled out a bottle that contained iodine.

"Who uses iodine nowadays?" he thought.

Jeremiah put a towel under her thigh and poured the liquid down the cut.

"Mother fu..," shouted Rebecca as she shot, bolt upright and punched the preacher in the face. His nose exploded, and blood sprayed all over Charlie's boots. A second later, the girl flopped back to the bed and passed out again.

"That looks nasty, boss," said the hitman, trying to fake concern and not to snigger with derision.

Jeremiah fell back onto the floor, desperately trying to jam two fingers up his nose to stem the bleeding and avoid incurring a penalty on his deposit. "Bitch," he screamed. "Kill her, shoot her, Charlie!"

"Boss, you are overreacting. It was just the iodine. She's out now. I'll finish cleaning her up, and she will be fine."

Charlie picked up a small wad of gauze and tipped the bottle upside down. The liquid pressed against the opening, slowly soaking into the material.

He carefully lowered it onto Rebecca's chest and wiped it up towards her collar bone. "Bastard!" she screamed and sprang upright again, swinging a punch at Charlie's face. Her fist was small, bony, and the perfect weapon to shatter the bridge of his nose. As soon as it connected, she passed out again.

Charlie jumped up, screaming. In a fluid movement, he pulled out a 9mm pistol and pressed it against her forehead.

"Not so funny now, is it, Charlie?" said Jeremiah. "I think you are overreacting now," Jeremiah used a pillow to soak up the blood. "Let her rest. You can kill her when I get the information I need."

"What about God?" said a voice in the darkness behind them.

The two men spun around, facing the shadowy corner of the room.

"What if God won't let you kill her, Jeremiah? Am I allowed to place a bet on that horse?"

A light switch clicked on, and a small man, dressed in a brown, black, orange and cerise striped soccer shirt, sat in a pool of light underneath a standard lamp.

"God, I assume," said Jeremiah, trying not to be shocked by his presence, "or whatever you are pretending to be today."

"If you want to use that name, it's ok."

"Why are you here?" asked the evangelist. "I guess you are not going to turn me to a pillar of salt, or you would have done it already."

"That's very old school," said Bill. "And as you are already a shower of shit, a pillar of salt would seem like a promotion for you."

"So why are you here, and what is that ridiculous shirt?"

Bill pulled the soccer top out in front of him. He looked down at the horizontal stripes. "This, Jeremiah, is the shirt from the first team to win the Football Association Cup in 1872. The team was called the Wanderers. Personally, I think of myself as a wanderer of sorts, so I adopted them as my home team. I watched every match they played from 1859 to their demise in 1887. Even the ones where the goal had no net or crossbar. Regardless of the weather, they turned up and pioneered a sport which binds a multitude of nations together around the world."

"Thank you for the history lesson. Now, you may leave unless you are intent on taking the girl from us bad men."

"I have not come to rescue Rebecca from you; I have come to rescue you from her. What do you think is going to happen when she finds out who you really are, Jeremiah?"

Charlie stood off to one side, continuously glancing around the room.

"Where's your friend?" he said.

"My friend?" said Bill.

"The one who keeps kicking me in the nuts. You can tell him I am going to break every bone in his body when I find him. Yeah, every bone."

Bill ignored the hitman's threat and, instead, stood up and walked over to the preacher. He stopped an inch from his face but a foot lower. "I have good news and bad Jeremiah" he said, looking up. "The good news is there is no such thing as hell. It doesn't matter how evil you are; you will not spend eternity roasting on a spit. The bad news is you have made an enemy of the wrong person."

The tall man looked down. "Oooh, scary. You won't kill me, and there is no hell. So I have no reason to worry about anything."

Bill leant back slightly, stepped onto the small box that had magically appeared at his feet, and head-butted Jeremiah in the nose. The big guy dropped onto the ground for the second time in an hour.

"Just because I show you compassion does not mean there are no consequences. I may not be the bloodthirsty God of the Old Testament, but don't mistake that for weakness." Bill stepped down, walked over to Rebecca and placed her arm over his shoulder. "I am not your problem; she is. You better leave her alone before she gets angry with you."

A loud pop rang through the room as Bill, Rebecca, and about ten cubic meters of air disappeared at the same time.

Charlie stood beside his Boss. "Do we really want to take on this guy?"

Jeremiah climbed to his feet, holding his nose and trying to stem the flow of blood. "If we want to fill my bank account from the wallets of gullible Christians out there in T.V. land, and you want a share of it, we don't have a choice. Anyway, you heard what he said. He will not do anything, and hell is not for us, so where is the risk?"

"What about the girl? He seemed very serious about her."

"Forget her, now, let's find the rest of his group and clean house. He is nothing without followers. Just a crazy interloper trying to fool the human race, the classic false prophet."

The two men walked into the bedroom and started unpacking a bag containing a startling array of riffles, pistols and grenades. "

It's time to put on our armour of faith, Charlie, not to mention packing an AR15 of retribution.

***

A petite Philippine nurse looked down at the white male in front of her. "He is very concussed. I think there may be some brain damage."

"By 'very' what do you mean?" said the middle-aged woman in surgical scrubs.

"He keeps asking where God is and if his dog is ok?"

"Is he sedated?" said the chief nurse.

"If we pumped him full of horse tranquillisers, he would be less stoned than he is now."

"So, to answer the question, where is his God and is his dog ok. Do we have them in the hospital?" said the doctor, looking at the fake I.D. hanging from her shirt. Her genuine I.D. was sitting in a locker at the local CIA office in town.

"Well, that is a difficult question." said the junior nurse. "First of all, which one are you talking about? Apolaki is the sun god from my country. If it's that one he is, as they say on the tin, the sun, so you can see him out of that window. If it's another, more modern or ancient one, it could be up to two and a half thousand different gods throughout history. Not to mention the 30,0000 Christian faiths. On top of those, there are 25 prophets of the Muslim faith that have fractured under more than 500 religious leaders. All of these lay claim to a personal insight into the Muslim understanding of God. And then there are all the Jewish faiths. Do you have a particular favourite?"

The CIA covert operative stared straight into the nurse's the eyes. Her question had not anticipated someone who understood the diversity of religious faiths and their connection to the political management of the proletariate. She leaned against the wall and re-evaluated the junior nurse. "Just this one," she said, holding up a poorly printed photo. "The short soccer fan in the news."

"Well," said the nurse, if you are limiting yourself to the one in the national media, he has not turned up since the young man arrived here."

"And the dog?"

"The T.V. pictures of the soccer fan holding one in his arms made it look like the dog was dead, unfortunately. Not surprising, though. Not many things take well to being blown up and then having parts of a building drop onto them."

The fake doctor picked up Mark's medical chart and pretended to read it. "What's his story?"

"I think he is lucky to be alive. Looks like a piece of masonry hit his shoulder and dislocated it. Another glanced off his head, leaving him with a severe concussion."

The doctor handed over a small white card with a phone number on it. "Because of the media interest, I have been asked by the Chief Medical Officer to keep an eye on his progress. He shouldn't have any visitors until I can talk to him and decide the best treatment. Call me when he wakes up and let me know if anyone tries to visit him." She turned, pushed the door wide and headed for the exit to report to her boss.

The petite nurse looked at the card and then dropped it into the bin. "You can come out now."

The door to the bathroom opened, and Marion walked into the room. Just behind her, Millie trotted into sight, wearing a small bandage around her right leg.

"Thank you," said the elderly lady. Other than a worried expression on her face when she sat on her son's bed and held his hand, she looked just as well as she did a day before.

"You are welcome," said the nurse. "We are on the same team." She pulled out a small crucifix on a chain around her neck.

"I don't know if we are," said Marion. "He seems a bit sketchy about the Jesus thing. It caught me by surprise, but I have come to terms with it now."

"You think he is the real deal?"

Marion hugged the younger woman. "I know he is, but that doesn't mean the Bible represents him particularly well. Even so, I still like him, and his heart is in the right place, assuming, of course, he has one."

The nurse hugged her back. "Let's give him the benefit of the doubt for now. I saw how upset he was when he was on T.V. carrying your little dog. Anyone that feels empathy for a dog is ok with me."

Marion cupped her son's cheek. The last time she had been this worried about him, he had been given the last rites when a nasty case of the croup confined him to bed when he was only five. "Is his concussion bad?"

"Bad enough to worry the specialist consultants." She watched Marion's concerned face. "Can't your friend fix it?"

"Apparently no. He says he can't or won't resurrect people and tries not to dabble in the micro details more than necessary.

"That sounds callous. It's not a hardship for him. A blink of an eye, and it's done."

"On Earth right now, there are 8 billion blinks walking around. The universe has thousands of other Earths, and there are a multitude of other universes. I think I get his thinking, even if I wish he would make an exception for my son," said Marion.

"Still, it's harsh. Perhaps I should look for a new god?" Marion looked down at Mark. Her face grew darker. "I don't think this is a horse race. We can't bet on another one. Bill is here, and he wants to help. From what he said, the life of my son is insignificant in comparison to what he is trying to help us achieve. As much as it tears me apart, I know Mark would be happy to give himself up if it meant a better future for the rest of us. He is a humanist. For him, it is all about about the greater good for all, not just for one."

"Who is Bill?"

"God prefers to be called Bill."

The nurse tipped her head to one side and considered asking why. Then she thought it would finish in the same dead-end street as the previous conversation and decided to just go with the flow. "I will keep close to your son. He will be ok if no one interferes. I can find you a place to stay here when you need to sleep. You will be safe for a few hours now until dinner tonight."
"Thank you. You are a good person." she looked down and read the nurse's name tag. "Jasmine."
"I wouldn't go that far, but I have a feeling I am on the right side of this argument," the nurse closed the door as she left. Marion sat on the side of the bed and held her son's hand. Marks colour was grey, and his eyes looked sunken. She didn't share the confidence the young nurse had. When Mark was a child, she had nursed him through many illnesses. Right now, he looked like he was sinking so deep she thought he might not make it back. If Bill changed his mind, it would be different but, after he transported her out of the apartment a millisecond before the bomb went off, he was very clear. When he went back to rescue the others, he warned her he would not bring them back if they had been killed. Even Mark.
"Marion," Bill had said, "I don't play God. It is one thing to help nudge Earth's future in a better direction but another to fight the natural laws the universe has successfully put in place. I have tried it before, and it gets very messy."

FOURTEEN

Rebecca opened her eyes and the bright sunshine hurt them just enough for her to lift her hand to her face. Instantly, the pain raced through her shoulder. "Oh god!" she hissed, as the white-hot ache became unbearable.

"Yes, Rebecca," said a voice at her feet.

She relaxed her arm so that she could see who was there. Sitting at the far end of the sofa she was lying on was Bill. He was wearing the same LA Galaxy soccer shirt her father used to wear.

"Nice touch, Bill. Maybe a little over the top, but I still appreciate the thought."

"I thought you might like it, how's the shoulder?"

"Excruciating."

"Then I suggest you don't put any weight on your leg yet either; that cut looks pretty nasty too."

To test the point, Rebecca lifted her thigh an inch or two off the sofa. The pain was not as bad as her shoulder, but it still hurt like hell. Except, she realised, there wasn't a hell. It was going to take a long while to get her head around the new world she was living in. She looked the small man in the eyes. "Bill, I never normally pray for divine intervention for myself but, as you are sitting there just drinking a mug of tea, perhaps you wouldn't mind healing me?"

"I told Marion I would not interfere with people's fate. I have tried it many times, and it always ends up creating a worse outcome."

"Oh good, a god with scruples. Just my luck. So why come here now if you are not prepared to get your hands dirty and help?"

"I came here for you."

"Me?" Rebecca ignored the pain and sat up. "What do you want with me. If you are looking for a new virgin for the second coming, I am afraid that ship has sailed."

"You people are really anchored to what is between the pages of the Bible, aren't you? You do realise it is a collection of stories, hearsay and anecdotes which contain a few facts that have been changed out of all recognition?"

"So Jesus was not your son?"

"It's too complicated to explain how everything happened back then. Suffice to say, I never met him, but, from what Mary told me about him, he was a fine young man and didn't deserve what happened too him."

"So you did meet his mother, Mary?" Rebecca adopted a conspiratorial whisper. "Like, you really knew her…?"

"You don't need to make it sound sordid. You have misunderstood. It was not that Mary. I meant Mary Magdalene. She is the important person."

Rebecca sounded disappointed. "Why her? She wasn't even a proper disciple."

"And this, Rebecca, is how stories get turned around over time. Mary was a very special person. I never had, in all of the worlds I had created, throughout any of the parallel universes, found a being that was like her. Pure, funny and with endless compassion. We spent a lot of time together. In fact, as much as we could."

"Without wanting to be labelled 'sordid' again, were you romantically involved?"

"For a short while. It was just before the crucifixion. I invited her to come with me to see all the worlds I had created. I was desperate to impress her, but she was too grounded for that. Mary was determined to do good in the world she had been born in. I knew I couldn't stay, so we said goodbye, and I left the day after the crucifixion." His face grew dark and sadness filled his eyes.

Rebecca slid closer and held his hand. She felt his loneliness as her fingers wrapped around his. "Did you see her again?"

"Once. I came back a few years later. Everything was confused. There were stories of a resurrection, and Mary had disappeared. Eventually, I found her. She was in hiding."

"What had happened?"

"A couple of days after I left, she had visited his body. The tradition was to wrap them in bandages with spices. Women or servants traditionally fulfilled the obligation. When she laid her hands on him, he suddenly took a breath. His wounds partly closed, and he sat up."

Rebecca sounded shocked. "But you said you didn't intervene."

"It wasn't me. It was her."

"How did Mary Magdalene suddenly develop God-like powers..?" Rebecca started, and the penny dropped. "She was pregnant, wasn't she? With your baby? It was the baby and not her."

"You are a smart young woman," said Bill, squeezing her hand.

"It's not smart; I felt it. I could see it somehow."

"You are very emphatic, Rebecca. It runs in the family." Bill left the words hanging in the air."

A second later, Rebecca snatched her hand away. "Oh no! No you don't. Don't tell me..?"

"What, that you are the latest in a long line of women who carry a unique genetic code? I won't tell you if you don't want me to?"

"So am I?"

Bill got up and walked to the kitchen. "You told me not to tell you," he said, as he pushed through the door.

Rebecca struggled to her feet. She suddenly realised they were in Mark's apartment. It was pristine, and there was absolutely no sign of an explosion.

"Bill, Bill!" she hobbled through the door after him. The pain enveloped her left side, but she ignored it as best she could. "Bill, seriously, who am I?"

He switched the kettle on and turned around.

"Honestly? Ok, Rebecca, you are the eighty-first daughter of Mary Magdalene."

"And you."

"Yes," said Bill. "And me."

She dropped into a chair at the table, partly because of her leg but mostly because her brain was struggling to make sense of what he said. "But I can't be. How could you have a baby with an earth woman?"

"Er, you do see the irony in that question. You were quite happy to think Jesus was my son but not that you are the descendant of a different Mary." Bill poured out two mugs of tea and carried them over to the table. He placed them side by side and knelt down in front of her. As he cupped her hands with his, he looked up into her eyes. "I told you you were special. Over the centuries, I have kept an eye on your family. Every one of your ancestors gave birth to a girl. Don't ask me why. Something about the genetic splice but all of them have been amazing people."

She dropped her gaze to the floor. "Bill, I'm not amazing, or perfect or pure."

"I never said you were perfect. Mary was as close to perfect as I ever witnessed. Far better than me. Even she wasn't perfect. You don't need to be to perfect to be exceptional. Watch." He lifted her good hand to her thigh and the deep cut running half its length. He placed it on top, and she felt the dampness of her own blood under her fingers.

"Take a deep breath," he said, "and imagine it as it was before the explosion."

"But…"

"Rebecca, just humour me."

She thought back to the day in the changing room where she had first tried on the red dress. As she changed, Rebecca had seen the nicely tanned colour of her legs. She tried to keep that image in her mind as she looked down at the destroyed skin above her knee. Her hand felt warm. Not warm, hot. It seemed that the heat was radiating outwards. Somehow she could see sinews biding deep inside, flesh fusing back together, and nerve endings reattaching. After a minute, it was perfect again. Even the blood was gone from the surface.

"How Bill?"

"When we have time, I will try to explain but, right now, you probably want to fix your shoulder. It looks dreadful."

"She moved her hand up to her arm and did the same thing. In five minutes, there wasn't a scratch on her."

She stood up. No pain. Nothing.

"Drink your tea," he said, "healing makes you feel dehydrated."

She sat back down and sipped the drink. As she put it down, she noticed her reflection in the glass of the oven door. Her dress was in shreds. "Can I fix this too?"

"It's more difficult here; let me help." He snapped his fingers, and the scarlet outfit instantly looked like it had just been taken off the rail.

"So, what now?"

Bill finished his tea. "Now we go to see our friend. Mark is not doing well."

"Bill?"

"Yes."

"Did you ever meet your daughter?"

"Yes, when I found Mary, she was being persecuted. The story of the resurrection was being co-opted by some of the men, and she did not care for the narrative. Worried about her daughter's safety, she decided to keep hidden for a while. When I caught up with her, our little girl was four."

"What was she like?"

"She glowed from the inside, metaphorically, of course. Beautiful and loving."

"And she had powers like me."

"Mostly. Every generation was slightly different."

"Bill, what was her name?"

He picked up the mugs and dropped them in the sink. "Why do you ask?"

"I think I know."

He turned back to her. "You ready to go?"

"Bill, what was her name?"

God lifted his hand and paused before he snapped his fingers. "Her name was Rebecca." and then, with a click, they were gone. The apartment slowly faded. Two walls were now missing, and part of the ceiling had been ripped off by the blast. The glass from the windows was scattered everywhere, and scorch marks ran up the external walls.

***

Aayan had woken up to a faint tap on his hotel door. He jumped out of bed and approached it naked, with a Glock 19 pointed in his outstretched hands. From a distance, he could just see under the door. A pile of papers were the only thing in view. As he arrived the evening before, he had ordered one of each national and local publications. He carefully opened the catch, made a gap just wide enough and dragged the pile inside. He guessed it was about twenty high. He usually made a point of scanning through them when he was on an assignment to gather intel. Usually, there would be something buried in one of them that would provide some helpful information. This time he didn't even need to open them. Each front page was covered with photos and type relating to his targets.

"Alien Antichrist Destroys Building" was the headline on the top of the pile. The next was very similar. The others devolved into a mixture of fear-mongering and sensationalism. None of them extolled the virtues of a visitation by God. He turned and placed them on the table in the middle of the room. After a quick search, he found the TV remote and started scanning through local and foreign news channels. Each one carried the same rhetoric. "My, how effective is the control of the media," he said out loud as he landed on a Russian speaking lady behind a large desk. Behind her, the graphics showed a badly photoshopped picture of the devil carrying a Stars and Stripes flag on a short pole. "Impressive," he thought.

Ayaan looked at his watch. "Time's nearly up, my old friend." He dropped the gun onto a large pile of munitions lying on the sofa and headed to the shower. This day could be very long or very short. Either way, he needed food, and American breakfasts were always impressive. Best not to miss the chance, so he determined to be quick getting ready. He did not relish killing Arsalan, but an order was an order. It would be better for everyone if he didn't take too long. Out of respect, he would make it fast and painless for his old friend. He just hoped he could convince him to repent before the end so that Arsalan could gain the rewards in heaven he deserved.

***

Mark's room's blinds were closed as Bill and Rebecca appeared with a muffled pop. It remained in semi-darkness. Through the closed bathroom door, a gentle whimpering stated. Bill swung it ajar, and Millie jumped into his arms and started licking his face. "Hello baby," he said, scratching her behind her ear, which made her tail wag uncontrollably. "I missed you too."

"You talk dog?" said Rebecca.

"I can scrape by," said Bill. "Anyway, it doesn't take a genius to see she is happy."

They both turned to look at Mark. His breath was shallow and slow. Rebecca sat on the bed and placed her hands on his chest. She closed her eyes and remembered him holding her in his arms. The way he felt, how safe she had been and the good heart she could hear beating in his chest. The warmth in her hands returned, and the strands of light from the window were enough to see the bruises disappear and cuts start to heal. His breathing strengthened, but his eyes remained closed.

"What's wrong, Bill? Why isn't he waking up?"

"Sometimes it just does not work like that. Mark took a lot of force to the head. He has damage you can't see, and that makes it harder. Try again."

"Can't you help? Just this once?"

"I am afraid this is literally in your hands."

Rebecca scowled at Bill before she looked back at Marks's face. Visually he seemed fine; in fact, he looked better than fine. He looked amazing. She held her hands on either side of his head. He was in there. She could feel it, but he was a long way down. Again the warmth returned to her palms, but he remained still.

"Bill!"

"Keep going. You can do it if you want to."

But she did want to. She wanted Mark back, and the thought surprised her. It was heartbreakingly real.

"You are not getting away that easily," she said and leant in and kissed him.

The room filled with light so bright it was impossible to keep watching. When it eventually faded, Rebecca was lying on the bed, and Mark was staring up at her.

"You know that could be termed as physical abuse," he said with a smile on his face. "Taking sexual advantage of a sleeping patient, I mean. I read somewhere Disney couldn't make a new version of Sleeping Beauty because Prince Charming would be locked up for common assault."

"Are you going to press charges?"

"Only if you don't do it again."

"That's blackmail."

"So we are both criminals." Mark lifted his head off the pillow and kissed Rebecca. There was no flash of light, but a certain amount of electricity filled the air.

"Can you two knock it off now? There is something very disconcerting about seeing you two together," said Bill, approaching the bed. "Anyway, you are embarrassing Jasmine."

Mark and Rebecca looked around the room, and a small lamp clicked on in the corner. A petite nurse sat transfixed in a chair. "I was just keeping an eye on you while your mother popped out to get a sandwich."

Bill walked over and place his hand on her shoulder. "And a great job you have been doing, Jasmine."

"You are God. Bathala, creator of all?"

"Er, just Bill, please just Bill."

Marion opened the door and stepped inside. As soon as she saw Mark sitting upright, she ran over and hugged him. After a minute, she realised Rebecca was lying on the bed.

"Did I miss something?"

Jasmine stood up. "The girl molested your sleeping son, but it seemed to do the trick, and now he is blackmailing her into giving him sexual favours."

"What?" said Marion.

"Don't worry it's all ok, said Bill."

"No Bill, it's not ok," said Marion. "And if she was your daughter, you would not be ok about it either. Finding a woman you hardly know laying on your dying son…"

"I'm not dying, mom, well not now anyway."

"Finding a woman you hardly know laying on your previously dying son…"

"You know her grandfather at least," said Bill.

"Well he must be morally irresponsible if he allows his granddaughter to throw herself at dying young men."

Rebecca smiled at Bill. "So it's your fault I am morally bankrupt."

Bill hung his head, shaking it gently.

"Why did she say that? What have you been up to, Bill?" Marion sounded like a mid 50's schoolmistress. "I'll tell you on the way, Marion, now you get off the bed, and you get up and get dressed. We have three floors to climb so that we can get Arsalan." Bill pushed Marion and Rebecca out of the door so that Mark could dress; he guessed that Jasmine had seen it all before.

***

Aayan had stolen some scrubs and attached his recently acquired ID to the collar. As he exited the locker room, he quickly made the fire stairs towards the side of the building. He made short work of the electronic catch and slid inside and onto the first set of steps. Arsalan was five storeys above him. It would only take a moment to inject him with the lethal dose of poison already in the syringe he had in his pocket. Just in case he had tucked the Glock into his belt loop. "No need to take chances," he thought.

On the second floor, the door flew open, knocking him into the wall and back down five stairs. In front of him, five people started running upwards. He recognised two of them. It was the small man pretending to be God and the American he had seen in the pictures. Shocked, it took him several seconds to register what was happening and, by the time he had cleared his head, they were two storeys above him. He hauled himself to his feet and ran after them.

Arsalan's door flew open, and suddenly the room was full of people. The young man was still full of painkillers and was only vaguely aware of what was happening. Initially, he had expected it to be his old

143

friend making good on his promise, but now a young girl was holding his shoulders. He suddenly became warm, and the room started to come into focus. His head cleared, and the pain stopped.

Rebecca looked down at him. "All good now?"

"Yes but how did..?"

The door burst open, and Ayaan raced in, reaching for his gun. As he swung it up to take aim, he pulled the trigger three times. The Nerf darts all bounced off of Arsalan's forehead and fell on the floor. "What the..?" He dropped the toy and reached for the syringe. Lifting it like a dagger, he ran for the bed. Mark grabbed his wrist and the two men slammed into the wall. Both men struggled to gain control.

Bill looked at Arsalan. "Can your friend swim?"

The young man shrugged.

"Let's find out." Bill snapped his fingers, and Ayaan disappeared. A mile out to sea, two fishermen heard a faint pop in the distance and watched a very angry man drop out of the sky and crash into the water. They turned their boat in his direction, but about twenty feet away, he was still shouting and stabbing the water with the syringe.

He spotted them and called out. "Hey, can you help me get to shore?"

"Absolutely," said the man at the wheel, "It's that-a-way about a mile." And he turned the boat around and headed in the opposite direction.

Ayaan decided it was going to be a long day and he was glad he had eaten well at the hotel. He started swimming in the rough direction of South Beach.

FIFTEEN

Cardinal Johnson was sitting in a large oak-panelled office that dripped of opulence beyond the norm. The only thing slightly out of place was the fake antique desk sitting in the middle. The rest of the decor was undoubtedly more extravagant than required in the office of a hospital administrator. But this was not any hospital, and Dr Jacobs was not any hospital administrator.

The surgeon had leant back in a large black leather desk chair staring at a file. "Father Paul is in stable condition. His broken arm has been set, and the bruising does not worry us at this time."

"Good Dr Jacobs, I am pleased to hear the excellent news."

Jacobs leant forward and peered over his glasses. "There is a problem with the police to consider, though. They should be notified he is here after surviving the bombing."

Johnson smiled. Here is where the bill gets padded, he thought. "The Church is, of course, very happy that we chose your facility for the Father to receive care. We know your confidentiality is second to none. I did, however, notice that your hospital could do with some charitable donations."

"We pride ourselves on providing good service for our patients, so any assistance is greatly received. What did you have in mind?"

The Cardinal leant back in his chair and rested his feet on the reproduction mahogany desk in front of him. "I am afraid the Church cannot make large cash grants, but I did notice we have a rather fine 16th-century desk in storage on our New York inventory. Perhaps it could be offered on permanent loan, under your personal care, of course, if you could find a use for it?"

Dr Jacobs eyed the cheap wooden top and then looked around the room. "The hospital would welcome such a kind offer, and I would vouch for its safety myself."

"Good," said the Cardinal, rising quickly, "now I would like to see the Father if that is possible."

"But the matter of the police, what..?"

Johnson cut across him. "I am in quite a hurry, lots of important God business to do, so shall we?"

He waved at the door suggesting the doctor should open it for him.

"Yes, of course. I will show you the way."

The two men strolled down one corridor and then up another to an area with large private suites.

"The father is in here," said the doctor with an overdramatic flourish of his hand.

The door swung wide, revealing a large bed with a small man sitting on it, drinking a mug of tea. On its side was a picture of John Lennon and the words "More popular than Jesus" written underneath.

The surgeon snapped his head around the room so fast he was in danger of needing a neck brace. "Who the hell are..?"

"It's ok Jacobs, I will deal with this," said Johnson, and he pushed the other man outside and closed the door.

"How's your boss?" said Bill, sipping his drink.

"His Holiness is fine, I believe. We have not spoken recently; I am handling this situation."

"By 'situation' you mean me?"

"Yes exactly. Your unwelcome arrival."

God stood his mug on the bedside table. "I thought you had been sitting around for 2000 years just waiting for my return."

"Yes, well, you are not living up to expectations; in fact, you are very disappointing."

"Why, because I did not arrive in Rome for a private audience?"

The Cardinal looked dejected. "Look, if you are the real God, then you must appreciate the effort we have been putting in since you left."

Bill stood up. "Cardinal, I know a little about your track record over the last two centuries. All I can say is that it hasn't been very Christian, and I am being kind, leaving it at that. There seems to be a major disjoint between the Church and what it stands for."

Johnson folded his arms. "Oh it's easy for you, isn't it. You disappear to God knows where for two millennia, leaving us looking after things, and then turn up and criticise us for the way we did it. A little thank you would be nice."

"You have some very good-hearted people in all the religions, but continually squabbling over which one is right is a waste of everyone's time. Not to mention the giant cash cow religion has become. Lots of individuals getting wealthy and powerful at the people's expense."

"See, it's that attitude that does not help."

"I don't like quoting from the Bible Cardinal, but maybe you should read Hebrews 4:12. In the meantime, talk to your boss; he should know what you are doing," and then Bill disappeared.

Johnson fished in his pocket and pulled out a small black Bible. He flicked through the pages and then read out loud. "Hebrews 4:12. 'For the word of God is living and active, sharper than any two-edged sword, piercing to the division of soul and of spirit, of joints and of marrow, and discerning the thoughts and intentions of the heart.'"

He put the Bible back in his pocket.

"Spiffing, absolutely spiffing. What is that supposed to mean?"

He walked outside, and Dr Jacobs was waiting.

"Should I call security?"

"No, it is all ok. Thank you for your help," he held out his hand.

The surgeon took it firmly and started to shake. Immediately the Cardinal's head filled with images of Jacobs smiling behind his surgical mask as he cut deep into a woman womb, a snigger as he turned off a life support machine, and the relish the doctor felt as he delivered a terminal cancer diagnosis.

Johnson recoiled and snatched his hand back in horror. "Discerning the thoughts and intentions of the heart," he said without realising it. "I have to leave now! Goodby Jacobs," and he nearly finished with 'good riddance'. He ran down the corridor and into the street, grateful to be in the sunshine. As he hurried across to his waiting limousine, a homeless lady caught his hand. "Could you spare a dollar, Mr or enough for a meal?"

Usually, the Cardinal hated freeloading street people. He had led the move to remove them from inside the Vatican walls. Now her tragic life spilled into his mind, complete with her emotions. The grief of a dead child. The loss of her true love and her slide into depression and bankruptcy.

He opened his wallet and handed her the contents. She gasped as she realised there were over a thousand dollars.

She began to cry as she looked at the cash. "God bless you, sir!"

"No thanks," he said, "not again."

As he slid into the rear of the car, the glass partition silently dropped down. "Where to, Cardinal Johnson?"

"A glove shop."

"Sir, this is Miami; I can't imagine they have any."

"Then to a Home Depot. They must have some workmen gloves, or welding gloves or gardening gloves. Anything."

The driver punched something into the satnav and slid the divider up, glad he was paid not to ask questions.

***

Sunset Key measures no more than 200 metres in any one direction. It is located a three-minute boat ride from Malory Square in Key West, which is the cocktail capital of the United States. In reality, Key West does not class itself as the United States at all and is locally thought of as The Conch Republic. If you would like to pickle your liver, there is no better place on Earth to start the process.

The Key is a man-made island with small properties starting at nearly 2 million dollars. If you want a beachfront building, you will get little change out of $10,000,000. Its most notable feature is not man-made. Each night, when the sun sets, the sky catches fire and people along the mainland applaud its beauty and toast it, of course.

As Bill popped into existence on the westerly beach, the rest of the group were already clapping as the sun dropped. Paul was handing out cocktails as fast as they magically appeared in his hands, and even Millie had a dog bowl with a Margarita in it.

At the last moment, as the sun was cut in half by the horizon, the sky turned into an orange inferno of colour. Everyone clapped louder and clinked glasses.

"Thank you," said Bill, standing behind them. "I put a lot of work into this place. Plus, the fishing is amazing."

Everyone turned around, and Father Paul stepped forward and offered Bill a Bellini. "You fish?"

God clinked glasses with him. "Yes, I fish. It is my favourite hobby but I hardly ever get the chance nowadays. In fact, the last time I had the opportunity was right here in 1934."

Mark stepped forward, gently kicking sand as he walked. "Wasn't Hemingway here then?" He clinked Bills glass and said, "cheers".

"Er yes. I gave him a cat."

Mark raised his eyebrows, immediately impressed.

"You gave Ernest Hemingway Snow White?"

"Who is Snow White?" said Rebecca, joining them and clanking her basketball-sized fishbowl of daiquiri against Bills.

Mark shook his head and slapped his forehead with his free palm. He looked down at her, smiling. "I just realised, you are a child compared to my age. My girlfriend is from the McDonalds generation."

Rebecca frowned. "The McDonalds generation? What is that supposed to mean?"

"If it's not available in two minutes, it's not worth waiting for and why learn stuff because it's all on Wikipedia now."

"Harsh," said Rebecca, "but fair. Although I would challenge you. Why do I need to keep filling my head with useless things which are instantly downloadable?"

"If you filled your head with these useless things, you would realise that Hemingway has a house full of six-toed cats. Apparently, a ship's captain gave him the original one; it was called Snow White."

"Best cat I ever had," said Bill. "He loved her as soon as he saw her, and I had such a great time fishing with him on Pilar, I just gave her to him."

Mark sank the rest of his drink and was immediately handed a new one by Paul. "You were on his fishing boat Pilar? Fishing? For fish?"

"Apparently. To be fair, I can't remember a lot about it; 1934 was a bit of a blur. We lived it up a bit. I treated it as a holiday and, anyway, he needed help with 'To Have and Have Not'."

Rebecca raised her hand to ask a question.

Mark shook his head and held her hand. "Don't ask, I'll give you a copy."

"Is it good?"

"One of the best pieces of modern literature ever written."

"You are welcome," said Bill. "Now, we have these two houses for the night. The important thing is to make a plan as to how we are going to change the future of your tiny planet. It's either that or this beach will be thirty feet underwater in the next two decades, and you lot will be fighting with the animals for the last grain of corn."

Marion and Arsalan stepped forward and clinked their glasses with Bill.

Rebecca noticed the giant Cosmopolitan in his hand. "You are drinking, Arsalan? I thought it was against your religion."

Everyone looked at Bill. "Don't ask me. I'm fine with it. This is what happens when you delegate important things. Gabriel is an archangel, but he is also a comedian and a bit lax when it comes to relaying detailed instructions. I mean, 72 virgins in paradise, how could he get that so wrong?"

"Good to know," said Arsalan after taking a drink, "glad you cleared in up thirteen hundred years down the road. At least it hasn't caused a problem in the meantime…"

"Don't start," said Bill, "Contrary to popular belief, I can't be everywhere."

"People management is not your strong point," said Marion, "First the Devil, now Gabriel. Perhaps you should review your recruitment policy."

Bill looked down crested. "Ok ok, I get it, I could have done better, but we are where we are. Now, let's focus."

"Can we focus over some food? I'm starving," said Rebecca.

"Good call," said Bill, happy to change the subject. "Dinner is served in the big bungalow. I think there is something for everyone."

They all walked up the beach and into the first property, which was now, miraculously, bathed in candlelight.

"Nice touch, Bill," said Mark, holding Rebecca's hand.

"I thought you two would appreciate it; now, let's eat." From the exterior, the large house on the beach looked amazing, but inside it was even better. Candles stood on every surface and lit the group's faces with puddles of light as they sat around the table. In the background, soft music was playing.

"I love soul," said Rebecca, sitting between Bill and Mark. She quickly squeezed both their hands to emphasise how much she was enjoying the evening.

"It's blues, not soul, I think," said Mark.

"I know this music, and it's definitely funk," said Paul. Bill leant forward to place his drink on the table.

"Actually, you are all correct. You all hear the music you personally like."

Marion placed a napkin on her lap. "Could we all hear the same one, Bill? I would like to share the same memories as everyone else if that's ok."

"Good call, mom. Whose do we choose?"

Arsalan stood up. "Can I suggest Rebecca's as three of us are only able to enjoy this because of what she did for us?"

Paul and Mark stood up as well. The Father picked up his glass. "And perhaps a toast before she explains how the hell she did what she did?"

Bill and Marion joined the rest. "To Rebecca, who gave me my son back and restored our friends."

Glasses clinked, and Rebecca blushed. As they sat down, a different dish appeared in front of each of them.

"I love lobster," said Paul and then looked at Arsalan's plate next to him. A large sandwich with rashers of bacon hanging out the sides sat in the middle. "Bacon, my friend?" he said, wrapping his arm around Arsalan's shoulder.

Both men were about the same age and, as they shared similar covert jobs, they had already built a conspiratorial bond.

"Father Paul, I have always wanted to try it. The smell is fantastic." He looked over at Bill, who nodded approval. Arsalan took a small bite to make certain a bolt of lightning wouldn't drop on his head. When he realised nothing had happened and that the taste was better than he imagined, he had another huge one to make certain. "Lubly," he tried to say as he chewed.

At the far end of the table, Millie was sitting in a babies' high chair, munching her way through a mountain of sausages. Next to her, Marion sat, watching Rebecca. The young girl was working her way through a giant slice of Black Forest Gateaux. Marion looked at Bill beside her, lit by the same candle. "It's the eyes," she said out loud. "Now I see you together, it's obvious. You both have the same eyes."

Everyone stopped eating and followed her gaze towards Bill and Rebecca.

"Santa Maria," said Paul, dropping his lobster. "I see it!"

Mark was still trying to finish his mouthful of burger. "See what?" he looked from Bill to Rebecca and then back again. The burger fell onto his plate. "When were you going to tell me, Bill, and exactly what am I looking at?"

"It wasn't that I did not want to tell you, Mark, I just thought Rebecca should be the first to know where her family's lineage started."

Mark stared at his girlfriend. "So are you a god too?"

"No, definitely not. From what I am told, my family only have girls, and each one has some abilities that they share with Bill. I seem to be very empathic and also have some healing capacity."

"So when did this all start?"

"About two thousand years ago."

Mark did the mental arithmetic and then snapped his head up to look at Bill. "That would mean you were around when…"

"Yes, her great great great… …anyway her grandmother knew him. I told you the Bible stories were a little confused in places."

"Confused! Confused!" shouted Paul. "We have been twisting ourselves in knots for two thousand years trying to make sense of how you were three people at the same time, and now we find out you weren't and that you had a girl, not a boy! No wonder the Church has been going crazy. Do they know?"

Bill put down his chicken wing. "There is a letter in a vault deep under the Vatican. It is from John the Apostle to James. It explains my relationship with Mary Magdalene, Rebecca's great grandmother." It was discovered in 1632 and taken to the holy city. By that time, St. Peter's Basilica had been built, and power and wealth were firmly in their hands. You can imagine why it was hidden."

"Does my boss know? Does Cardinal Johnson know?"

"Yes, the inter sanctum all know. It is their biggest secret. A couple of Popes who were told decided they would let the world know. Unfortunately, they unexpectedly died before they had the chance."

Paul picked up his drink, sank the lot and threw the glass over his shoulder. It disappeared before it hit the floor and another appeared in his hand. He repeated it twice more and then decided his liver couldn't manage a fourth. "I have spent my career supporting a bunch of conmen."

"To be fair, Paul, The Current Pope does not know. They stopped telling the new ones because it was so much trouble replacing them."

Arsalan leant forward. "Anything I should know about my religion?"

"No, you are pretty ok, I guess. Any issues you have is with people's interpretation and Gabriel's bad communication skills," said Bill.

Marion was still watching Rebecca. "Although I am a little disconcerted about Bill's revelation, I am glad you are here, Rebecca. Mark has needed someone spiritual in his life for a long time, and I'm pleased it's you."

"Mom please, not in front of everyone."

"Quiet Mark, mom knows best," said Bill, laughing. When he eventually stopped, he grew serious. "Now we need to make a plan. I feel like we are behind the curve, and there is a large queue of people forming that do not have our best interests at heart."

Rebecca leant forward. "I have been thinking. At the moment, the bad guys are controlling the narrative in the media. We need to get on top of it. P.R. has to be our first objective."

"I have a contact number for a friend at the affiliated news station in Miami," said Mark. He pulled out his mobile, searched through the address book and pressed go. He switched it to the speaker and handed it to Bill. After a few rings, a woman's voice answered. "Hello tiger, long time no talk, darling."
Rebecca shot a black look at Mark, who shrugged his shoulders. Across the table, Marion stared at her son and shook her head in disapproval.
"It's not tiger, he's busy. It's God, and we need to chat."

***

Sarah Golding pressed end on her phone. When Mark's number flashed up, she was excited. They had only had a few casual dates while she was working on a series of stories about public broadcast stations, and she had interviewed him several times. He had made quite an impression, but work had meant there had not been any communication in over two months. Perhaps he was calling to invite her on another date.
When a different voice spoke and said he was God, her initial suspicion was one of his friend's had got hold of his phone. Before the end of the first sentence, she realised it was serious.
Now she had to decide what the best plan was. She had been stuck in the same reporter's job for three years and was desperate to secure an anchor's position here, or better still, at a national station. This opportunity was too good to miss. She flicked through her contacts and eventually stopped at a woman's name with a star after it. Sarah had met Caroline Black at a cocktail party for writers in New York the year before. She was Program Director of one of the country's largest news networks. Although she was not

used to dating women, the two somehow ended up back at Caroline's apartment, and she woke up the following day next to a note on the pillow. It said 'Thanks for last night, you were wonderful x. Had an early morning meeting, so had to leave. Help yourself to breakfast and call me if you are in New York again and would love to meet up'. After it was a mobile number with a heart circling it.

Sarah dialled her number.

"Hello, Caroline Black."

"Hi Caroline, it's Sarah, we met…"

An excited voice cut her off. "Sarah, wow, so glad you called. Are you in town? It's late, but I can meet you. Where are you?"

"Miami."

The voice sounded disappointed. "Oh that's a shame."

"Listen, Caroline, I would love to meet up again, but I am calling about business. If you like what I tell you, I could be in New York tomorrow."

The voice perked up again. "Tomorrow works; what did you have in mind?"

"I need a thirty-minute prime time slot for an interview."

"Sarah, we can't just drop the schedule and make a new one. Anyway, we would have to use one of our team to do the interview."

"Can any of them get an interview with God?"

The line went quiet for a while. "Are you telling me you can get this God character in the studio?"

"On condition I do the interview and am guaranteed a co-anchor's trial, I can get him there tomorrow night."

Caroline was faced with the easiest decision of her career. A world exclusive with God and an excuse to bring Sarah to New York for the next few months at least. "Deal. You will be on air at 7pm. Send me your flight details, and I will arrange a limo."

"Apparently we won't be flying. He said he will sort it out, but if you could arrange a hotel with 6 rooms that take a dog."

"There will be six of you?"

"Seven."

"Why only six rooms?"

"I thought I could stay at yours."

Caroline beamed at the phone. "See you tomorrow." She put down the phone with her head spinning with ideas. Some work-related, but most about Sarah. Eventually, she calmed down and started dialling numbers. Within twenty minutes, the schedule was changed and a studio booked.

Tomorrow may be the best day of her life so far.

SIXTEEN

After President Goncharov and Alexi Lebedev had landed at Langley, they had been completely hidden from the American public. Within an hour, they choppered to CIA headquarters and were now in a secure meeting room. Goncharov's security team had swept the area twice. The first time highlighting 27 surveillance devices. Two hours later, huge holes in the plaster walls and ripped out electrical outlets were re-scanned for additional devices. When everything received a green light, Alexi confirmed the meeting with his boss could go ahead.

In a separate room, a CIA official leant around the door. "President Jeffries, Goncharov is happy to meet you now."

Jeffries shook his head in disappointment. "The leader of the free world waiting for little more than a jumped-up gangland thug to summon him. What is the world coming to?"

He stood up and followed the bald man in a classic black CIA suit down the hall. As he entered the meeting room, Alexi got up and shook the President's hand. He was slightly taken aback when he realised he was holding a small yellow duck that looked like an American Eagle. "It is an honour to meet you, sir," he said, looking at the small toy. "My name is Alexi, and this is…"

Goncharov finished Lebedev's sentence "…the jumped up gangland thug. Yes, we have met before, Alexi. As my friend here has said on TV, 'let's cut the crap'."

Jeffries looked suspiciously around the room. "How did you..?"

"Unlike you, President Jeffries, my team treat every location as hostile and sweep for bugs, even our own offices. Would you like me to tell you the colour of your girlfriend's panties you are wearing right now?"

Jeffries turned scarlet for a second before recovering his composure. "And would you like me to give you the account numbers and passwords of your Swiss bank accounts?"

"Well managed, my friend. Alexi, do the honours."

Jeffries was taken aback by being called a friend by the Russian, but, given the circumstances, they were comrades at least.

Lebedev opened a leather case and lifted out a bottle of Wild Turkey Diamond Anniversary and three large shot glasses.

The American watched as Alexi poured each one full. "You know, Mr Goncharov, I fail to understand why we have never done this before?" He picked up a glass and emptied it in one go.

Alexi immediately refilled it.

The Russian President picked up his glass. "I think it may have to do with the fact that each of us has nearly 7,000 nuclear warheads pointed at the other and, up until now, we did not have a shared enemy." He downed the shot, and immediately Alexi topped it up.

"It is good to see you again so soon," said Jeffries, extending his hand.

Goncharov did the same but, instead of holding flesh, he ended up with a plastic duck dressed up in a chicken suit. "Er, Mr President, I did not bring a gift for you."

"Funny. Wait until God catches up with you. I can't wait to see what he plagues you with." As he turned around Goncharov's suit turned into a Bo-Peep outfit complete with bonnet and crook.

"Oh that's not good," said Jeffries.

The Russian looked at his subordinate. "What? Alexi what? Tell me man!"

Lebedev considered the options. Shoot himself in the head now or tell the truth. Alexi felt in his pocket for a gun, but he had left it on the plane. No choice then. He pulled out a phone and took a photo of his boss, and then turned it around so he could see.

"Chyort!" shouted Goncharov.

Jeffries waved his hands to try and calm his counterpart down. With each shake, another duck flew into the air. By the time he stopped, the Russian was surrounded by rubber ducks dressed as sheep.

Prime Minister Goncharov looked at the flock around his feet. "You did this," he screamed as he jumped to his feet. "We will destroy this little god with our most powerful weapons!"

Images of a thousand nuclear warheads dropping on Miami blasted into Jeffries's head. "No! We will find him and deal with him another way. We just need intel on where he will be, and then we can set up a kill zone that even this God cannot avoid. We must deploy all our agents and leave no stone unturned until we find this person, however long it takes."

The door opened, and a CIA agent walked in. "Sir, perhaps you would like to turn on the news broadcast. You and the Batman may be interested."

Jeffries looked in the direction of the agent's stare. Goncharov was now wearing a black cape and mask.

He turned back. "Thank you, how do we get the television on?"

The agent grabbed a small remote off the wall and clicked it once. A second later, an advert was rolling on the screen, and a voiceover started talking. "Tonight at seven, God talks exclusively to the News Network." In the background, images of a bearded giant floating in the clouds filled the screen. "Our new Co-Anchor, Sarah Golding, will be live in our New York studio to ask the questions you want answering. Alien insurgent or loving deity, you decide."

The two Presidents looked at each other and smiled. "Alexi, we need another drink to celebrate."

Lebedev poured them both another shot and then called a number on his phone.

"Yes, our friend needs to leave Miami and be in New York this afternoon." He stopped the call.

"Our asset will be in place, Mr President."

In unison, both men said, "thank you".

***

In Miami, Sarah Golding walked out of her station's head office. She had wanted to tell her boss that she was resigning before he heard it elsewhere. Unfortunately, she hadn't bargained on Caroline's efficiency. Sarah saw the first advert while she picked up her first coffee of the day. On the wall in the corner was a muted television with rolling subtitles. Filling the screen was a publicity shot of her that Caroline's team must have pulled off the internet. The man in the front of the queue turned and said, "Do you really know God?"

"We have spoken once."

"Can you ask him what next week's lottery numbers will be and tell him to text Jim Marshal?"

"I'll see what I can do," she said politely and picked up her coffee and left.

By the time she got to the studio, a wall of a dozen news crews were waiting. She drove past and parked in a side street, and entered through a quiet rear entrance. As she passed through the building, small groups of colleagues whispered and pointed. It was the first time they had ever really noticed her, and she loved it. After a heated discussion with her boss, which finished with an empty threat that 'she would never work in this town again', she left the same way.

As Sarah slipped behind the wheel of her car, she checked the time on the dashboard. 7:30. At this time of day, she should be in Key West by 11am. When she had talked to God, her only condition was that they meet before going to New York. There was no way they were walking into a studio where she could jeopardise her new career unless they had a clear understanding of what was required. She pressed the start button on the BMW, slid her sunglasses from the top of her head down over her eyes and pointed the car south.

As it made the turn at the end of the street, a black Camaro with darkened windows pulled out behind her at a safe distance. At the intersection, it took the same turn again, and both vehicles accelerated onto US Route 1, heading to the Keys.

***

"We have had an idea," said Arsalan, striding alongside Father Paul and into the room where everyone was having breakfast.

"And what is that?" said Bill, sipping a black coffee. Paul poured himself one and continued, "Well, we have a certain set of skills and are feeling a bit

163

redundant at the moment. It's not in our nature to sit around, and we believe we can be more pro-active." Bill topped up his coffee like he was pouring the most precious liquid in the universe. "What do you suggest?"

Arsalan took over, "Well, we have guessed that you can't see everything that is going to happen yet. You seem to be very reactive in the moment. Is that fair?"

Bill smiled, "Yes, that is true. I have some ability in the moment, but if I want to see what is going to happen, I have to travel to the future and then come back and change it. The problem you have is that once you change one thing, everything has changed, so you end up having to bounce back and forth. Ultimately it never achieves everything you want, so I stopped doing it. My empathic feelings let me know some things are about to happen, but not all. When the bomb went off, I had a glimpse of someone saying my name. It was the guard downstairs that was blown up in the van. Even then, I only had time to transport Marion to safety."

"We sort of put that bit together," said Paul, "so we have an idea to get ahead of our enemies. As part of our old jobs, we both have access to various assets hidden locally. For instance, we both have safe houses available if we need them. Our two in Miami are only three streets away from each other, and they both have links to our security networks where we can find out what is being planned for us. If we leave quickly, we can be there and back by the time you transport us to New York."

"I could just transport you to the houses, and you could be there and back in an hour," said Bill.

"Yes, we thought about that," said Arsalan, "but then we are stuck doing nothing again. We suggest a road

trip for the two of us. It would keep us busy and hopefully provide good intel; what do you think?"
"Does it matter what I think? You boys have already made up your minds."
The pair looks at each other and nodded. "Yes, we have, said Paul, "but it would make life easier if we had a car. Something sporty?"
Both men smiled as sweetly as possible.
"Go, it will be on the quay when you get to the mainland. Be careful."
"Thanks, Bill," and they both ran for the door.
An hour later, they were stepping off the tiny ferry boat and onto the dock. As they walked up the wooden gangway, they passed a good looking woman wearing sunglasses heading in the opposite direction.
"My name is Sarah Golding," she said to the small lady captaining the craft. "I have a meeting with one of your guests on the island. His name is Bill, I believe."
The small lady checked her clipboard and waved for her to climb aboard. Sarah chose a seat near the far side, sat down and started writing some notes.
Back on the quay, the two young men were pleased with Bill's choice of ride. It was dead easy to spot the car he had provided. A brand new electric blue Shelby Mustang with a double white stripe over the roof and down the hood was parked under a palm tree on the sidewalk.
"Cool," they said in unison, racing to be the first to the driver's door. Paul was just ahead and shouted over his shoulder, "You can drive back."
"Deal."
Paul threw a small rucksack into the back and picked up the key on the seat. As the car roared into life and screeched onto the street, their laughter could be heard until they made the first turn.

The sound of the Mustangs engine drowned out the sound of Aayan starting the Black Camaro and turning to follow them. It had been a surprise when the female reporter had parked her BMW at the end of the side street and walked to the boat. It was even more of a surprise to see Arsalan and the priest climb into the blue car and drive off. Now he could see his prey, and he was in no hurry to catch him. There was only one road out of town all the way and ran to the end of the Keys. He could catch up to them in a mile or two and keep a safe distance until he worked out where they were heading.

"Time's running out, my old friend," he said and accelerated towards the first bridge at the end of the island.

Back on Sunset Key, Bill stood in the doorway of the large bungalow watching Sarah Golding disembark the boat, get directions at the end of the quay and start walking along the beach towards him. By the time she stepped onto the porch, she was feeling the heat. It was a stunning day with blue sky from horizon to horizon, and she was happy to feel the cool air from the air conditioning blowing through the door past Bill.

"Hello Sarah, good to meet you, I'm Bill," he stepped forward and shook her hand.

She gasped as he held her, and waves of calm swept over her. Suddenly the beautiful sky became iridescent, and she pitched sideways, overwhelmed with the emotions racing through her.

Bill caught her and lowered her into one of the rattan chairs on the deck. "It will pass in a minute," he said.

"I don't want it to," Sarah said, surprising herself at being so open.

Mark appeared at the door carrying Millie and followed by Rebecca a foot behind him.

Sarah looked up and smiled. "Hello tiger, long time no see."

Mark was about to return the smile when sharp fingernails dug into his right buttock. He took the hint and turned his wide smile into a polite grin. "Hi Sarah, I see you have met Bill already. That first handshake is a bit overwhelming, isn't it?"

She looked at the little man. "So it's true, you are The God?"

"If you mean the one that created this universe, then yes," Bill said, pouring her a glass of iced lemonade from a jug that had suddenly appeared in his hand.

Mark jumped in. "Actually, I pressed the start button on the universe. It was only symbolic but still really cool."

Sarah was already out of her depth in the conversation, which had become really weird really fast. "What was it like?"

"Not as noisy as you would think. Big flash, and then everything began accelerating into the distance," he said, sitting in the chair next to Sarah. There was nowhere left for Rebecca, so she took the opportunity to sit on his lap and throw an arm around Marks' shoulder.

He looked a little embarrassed and realised he hadn't even introduced them. "Sarah, this is Rebecca. She is Bill's…"

"…friend and Mark's girlfriend," finished Rebecca. At this stage, she was still coming to terms with the news that she was related to Bill and thought now was not the right time to reveal herself to the world at large. Especially by a reporter who had some sort of relationship with her boyfriend.

Millie broke the tension by jumping out of Marks's arms and onto Sarah's lap. Rebecca took the opportunity to snuggle further onto his lap into the space the little dog had left.

"And who are you?" said Sarah, instantly ingratiating herself by scratching the Dachshund behind her ears. Bill did the same, "This is Millie, and you will be her friend for life if you keep doing that. Now, Sarah, I am guessing you have some questions for me. Where would you like to start?"

She stopped scratching the dog, reached into her bag and pulled out a thick wad of papers. Each one was full of blue bullet-points written in small, neat handwriting. A question mark hung at the end of each line.

Sarah looked up, "I have one or two," she smiled and began at the top of the first page.

***

Two hours later, Father Paul pulled up outside a small but beautifully built detached house a few blocks from Miamis south beach. Arsalan looked out of the side window. "Wow, you can tell which of our religions has more cash."

Paul turned off the engine and climbed out of the driving seat. "This is a conservative one. In most major capitals, we have a fully-staffed facility. This one is unmanned and completely off the books."

At the gate, he slid a key card into a slot and the building came to life. Electrical devices sprang into action, and the motor on the steel gates hummed as it dragged the metal back.

Paul slid behind the wheel, pulled the car in and drove up to the door. As they approached, it automatically opened and the two men strode in, pushing it closed behind them. The interior was luxurious in a subtle way that only Italian decorators can achieve. Arsalan guessed it doubled as a residence if any high ranking official was in town.

Both men stopped dead in their tracks. Sitting on the table was a copy of this morning's newspaper. Guns immediately appeared in their hands and, as if choreographed, they worked from room to room. Eventually, they made it to the master bedroom.

In the trash can, Paul found a copy of an Italian luggage tag with the Cardinal's name on it. 'Johnson must be using the place while he is in town,' he thought. But where is he now? As if in response, Arsalan walked over with a piece of notepaper from the bedside table. On it was a flight number and a time with the letters JFK after them. "He's flown to New York. Must have seen the news channel this morning and found out we would be there tonight."

"Good," said Paul, "We can still stick to the plan." He walked down to the ground floor and then opened the basement door. At the bottom of the steps, he turned right and ended up at a wall covered in shelves. On the top one, he felt along and found the small button. As he pressed it, the whole unit, including the wall, swung to one side. Lights immediately flash on, and suddenly they were entering a new room. Along one side a mixture of weapons and other equipment. On the other was a long desk with three screens and keyboards. Paul sat down and started typing a password. He pressed enter and a security notice flashed up, letting him know it was incorrect. He tried again, and the same thing happened. "They have shut me out."

Arsalan leant over his shoulder and started typing. As he pressed enter, the screen turned into a query page. "We have had access to your network for over a year now."

Paul's initial reaction was one of horror but, under the current circumstances, it soon turned into amusement. He began searching communications sent in the last two days. To start with, there were hundreds of questions flooding in from the different countries covered by regional offices. Then yesterday, a single message stopped everything dead. It said simply, 'Until further notice, communication with the media is not allowed and all requests for comment should be directed at Cardinal Johnson's office in Rome.'

From then on, only a single email had been sent informing the offices of a significant concern based on intelligence gained by the US government as to the nature of the Alien the American government believed was blasphemously masquerading as the second coming. It mentioned that the Russian authorities were working closely with them to ascertain what the individual's objective was. It promised more details as soon as they were available.

After that, nothing.

"It looks like my boss is keeping a distance and letting others do his dirty work."

"It did make me wonder where our information came from. I was dispatched so quickly it felt like we had suddenly been given intelligence that meant the only option we had was to pull me off a top priority project. We didn't have to get a team in place, and I was the only one who could react fast enough. Maybe the Cardinal is pulling many strings."

Paul nodded. "Given what is at stake for the church, this may be the only way they can play a role without committing themselves. Better to wait and see how best to manage the situation as it unfolds. Having you eliminate everyone would have been a double win for him. If it went well, he could expose your part in it and condemn your faith; if it went badly, his hands would still be clean."

"Tricky but clever. We must not underestimate him. Now, do you mind if I borrow some of the equipment back there?"

"Help yourself," said Paul, "as you implied, my organisation has deep pockets."

Arsalan grabbed two boxes of shells, a taser and a small briefcase he guessed contained a rifle with a scope. "Just in case," he said.

Paul picked up several ammunition clips and followed him back into the main house.

Outside he threw the car keys to Arsalan. "Your turn, my friend." The two of them grinned like children, climbed into the car and headed for the other safe house. When they arrived, it was a distinctly different neighbourhood. As they pulled up to the mid-terrace building, Arsalan looked embarrassed at the stark contrast to the previous house. There was no drive, so they had to park at the curb, about three car lengths' back.

The two men climbed out and headed for the door. Behind them, the black Camaro slowed to a stop fifty feet away. As they approached the steps, Arsalan took the lead and walked into the doorway.

In the Camaro, Aayan pulled a phone out of his pocket. It only contained one number. As they got to the door, he pressed send.

"Stupid," said Arsalan, "I need the key code from my phone; wait a second." He jumped down the steps and clicked the remote to open the Mustang. He picked up his phone from the centre console and turned back. Paul had leant against the door and watched his friend retrieve the device, just as he heard a phone ring immediately on the other side of the door. Arsalan was a few yards away when Paul realised what it was. "He shot forward towards the street and screamed, "Back!" just as the signal from the phone ignited the explosives Aayan had planted inside the door.

From where Arsalan was, he only saw the Father leap toward him and shout the warning. Next, the front of the building erupted, engulfing Paul and vaporising his body. Arsalan was thrown backwards, partially shielded by a large tree on the sidewalk.

His body landed on the hood of the car, and he was close to unconsciousness when he saw a familiar face above him. It was Aayan, and he was pointing a gun at his forehead. "Goodbye old friend," and he pulled the trigger. The bullet ripped into the metal of the car and left a neat hole in the paintwork. Arsalan's body had gone.

Aayan spun around, but he was the only person on the street. He turned back to the car and shot it another five times before he stormed back to his car and drove towards Miami airport.

SEVENTEEN

Arsalan opened his eyes. Rebecca was standing over him with her hands on his chest. She smiled as his focus improved, and then she slid to the ground next to him.

"Rebecca!" shouted Mark. He scooped her up and laid her on the sofa. "Bill, what's wrong with here?

"Arsalan was very badly hurt. The closer to death someone is, the more it takes out of her to repair the damage." Bill took her hand as she opened her eyes again. "She'll be ok, Mark. She just needs some rest for a while."

Arsalan jumped up, "Paul!"

Bill put his hand on his shoulder. "I'm afraid he's gone. When the bomb went off, I felt him call out but too late. But I did manage to get you. He saved your life."

Arsalan sat back down and buried his head in his hands. "It was my fault. I should have guessed."

"How could you know? No one could, not even me. There is no point playing the 'what if' game. He did something good with his life; he saved you, now you have to make certain you do good things with yours."

"My first good thing will be to kill Aayan."

"That's not what I had in mind," said Bill.

"Then what?"

"You will work it out."

Arsalan looked over to Rebecca. She appeared pale and drained.

He sat beside her and said, "Thank you again. Did it hurt when you healed me?"

"You were nearly gone. I could feel you slipping away. It took everything I had to stop you. If you could avoid being blown up again, that would be great. You seem to be making a habit of it."

For a second he smiled, and then the image of Paul being enveloped by the blast swam back into his head. It had looked like the building was an angry monster and swallowed him whole.

His smile disappeared, "Thanks again," and he walked out onto the beach to be alone with his thoughts.

Sarah came through from the kitchen, carrying a mug of tea. She sat next to Rebecca and handed it to her. "I thought this might help."

Although the young woman didn't like the thought of Sarah with her boyfriend, she appreciated the idea and carefully took the drink.

The reporter stared at the stunning woman in the red dress. She was truly beautiful, but there was something else. When Arsalan had suddenly appeared on the floor in front of her, bloody, unconscious, and near death, she had watched Rebecca as she lay her hands on his chest. For a few seconds, the room blazed with light and then the girl collapsed. A moment later, the dead looking man was talking.

"How did you do that? He was dead. Now he's walking around."

"No, he wasn't quite. Dead is dead; I have no power to change that. Nearly dead I can work with."

"But how..?"

"Look, you have a great story here with Bill. Please do not mention me. I am still coming to terms with this, whatever it is, and I am not ready to be judged by a world that will be wary of something this different."

Sarah's natural instinct was to pursue a story this big.

Mark sat on the arm of the sofa. "We would both appreciate it and, I am certain if Rebecca ever decides the time is right to talk, you will be the first person she calls."

The reporter looked at the couple as they held hands. Mark had given her the biggest story in modern history. She thought, what the hell. "I promise not to mention what I saw. An exclusive with God will probably keep my career going for a while." She took the empty mug from Rebecca and returned it to the kitchen.

Mark wrapped his arms around his girlfriend. "Now, cut the B.S. How are you really?"

Rebecca had been playing down the impact saving Arsalan had had on her body. In the end, it felt like she would never recover. When she felt him return, she was nearly at the point of no return. It had almost cost her everything. Mark deserved to hear the truth. "Not good. It was a close call."

"How close?"

Rebecca looked up and kissed him but said nothing. "That close. No more, Rebecca. I just found you; this is not the time to go and kill yourself. Ok?"

She liked him caring that much. She let him hold her tight. "Ok, I promise I will not take any stupid risks."

"That's not exactly what I wanted to hear, but it will do for now. Expect me to stick to you like glue until this thing is sorted."

"Oh if I must," she said and kissed him again.

Sarah walked in, realised she was interrupting a moment and promptly turned around and left again. She found Bill talking to Marion outside.

"I think we should reconsider this interview, Bill. Everyone knows where we are going to be and when. You can't protect us all. Father Paul is testimony to that."

Bill hung his head. He was disappointed he had let the young man down. "No one knows the risks we are taking more than me, Marion, but we have no choice. The thought of us failing far outweighs any price we have to pay. Perhaps I should go to New York on my own."

"That is not what I meant. If you decide to go, we are going with you, and that's the end of it. What I thought was maybe changing the venue or day and only doing it at the last minute."

Bill looked at Sarah, who had been quietly listening. "That will not work, will it, Sarah? The only way we will reach the maximum audience is if it is advertised in advance. Isn't that right?"

The blond reporter nodded. "Bill's right Marion. It has to be advertised, and it has to go out live, or it can be edited to represent whatever narrative the people want to portray."

"So we have no choice. In which case we should arrive early. Better we surprise anyone waiting for us rather than have them surprise us. When are we expected at the studio?"

Sarah thought about it. "Maybe five-thirty. It will give us two hours in wardrobe and hair and makeup."

"We have another option," said Bill, "we could go to the hotel now and wait until the last minute to arrive. You could go ahead and prepare everything. We do not need hair and makeup," Bill stood up, and Sarah gasped.

In front of her, he was now dressed in a replica of Charlton Heston's costume from The Ten Commandments, and he was definitely five inches taller.

Marion burst out laughing. "Now that looks more the part. All you need is the voice."

As if on cue, a booming voice came from every direction.

"And I will strike down upon thee,
With great vengeance and furious anger,
Those who attempt to poison and destroy my brothers,
And you will know my name is the Lord".

As the last syllables reached a crescendo, the windows rattled and a picture fell off the wall. Arsalan leapt onto the veranda, brandishing a gun and looking for the source of the noise. "What is happening?" he shouted over the echoes of the last syllables.

Mark and Rebecca appeared through the door. "Who is the Tarantino fan that scared the hell out of Millie?"

"I believe Tarantino was quoting me," said Bill, "but to be fair, I have never threatened to strike down anyone with great vengeance. I might have had a harsh word with a few people, but you can see how these things get blown out of proportion over time." Bill put his arm around Arsalan's shoulder. "I understand you are very angry at the moment, but you can't start shooting everyone, ok?"

The young man holstered the gun and shrugged. "I will do my best, but I can't promise anything."

Sarah stepped forward, "er Bill, are you really planning to go on television looking like that?"

"You think it's too much?" but before she could answer, he was back in a soccer shirt and jeans. It was in the Brazilian national team's colours and on the back it said 'PELE 10'.

"Better," she said. "Ok, so they have booked six rooms for you guys at the hotel, and you can go there whenever you are ready."

"Five," said Arsalan.

It dawned on them that they would need one fewer reservations. Arsalan's survival had masked the loss of

Paul. The mood grew dark, and everyone melted away except for Sarah. "Can you get me to this address," she said, handing Bill a note with Caroline's details on it.
"You are looking forward to seeing your friend?"
Sarah nodded, slightly embarrassed.
"No need to be coy; I think it's nice. You know Caroline really likes you?"
"How do you know that?"
He turned around, and Pele's name had disappeared from the back of the shirt. Now it said 'GOD'.
"Oh yeah," she said.
"Give her my regards and see you tonight at the studio."
He snapped his fingers and she appeared in Caroline's apartment, sitting next to her on the sofa. Caroline screamed, dropped her coffee and fainted. "This is going to be a long evening," said Sarah, heading for the bathroom cabinet to look for some smelling salts.

**

"This is going going to be a long evening," said Bill as he, Marion, Arsalan, Mark and Rebecca appeared on the top floor of the New York hotel; each had a key card in their hand. "It's 3pm. Have some rest, and I will let you know when we need to leave. Arsalan and Marion let themselves into rooms on opposite sides of the hall.
Bill picked up Millie, "Do you mind if I take her, I thought I could feed her and maybe play a while?"
"Please do; she must be hungry."
Bill didn't bother opening the door but just disappeared with the dog in his arms.
Rebecca looked at Mark. "What room are you in?"
"The one next to my mom."

"I'm in the one at the far end. The one where Marion will not be able to hear your screams from?"

"Why would I be in your room screaming?"

"For mercy," she said, leaning against the door frame for a second and comedically fluttering her eyelashes before gliding into the room.

As the door was about to swing shut, he ran through the gap behind her, and the hallway fell silent…

…until the screams for mercy started.

EIGHTEEN

The situation room, buried deep under The Whitehouse, was usually a hive of activity in times of national emergency. Today, the large meeting table only had three people sitting around it.

President Jeffries, Alexi Lebedev and a cowboy.

The large digital screen on the wall had most of its fantastic functionality switched off. It usually could display everything from live satellite feeds to the trajectories of incoming nuclear warheads. Today it just told the time. A large red on black display read 15:53.

They all sat waiting in silence until it showed 16:02 and the door open to allow Harry Jacobs inside with a tray of coffee and a large file under his arm.

He placed a cup in front of each man and then sat down a few places away from his President. As he did, he noticed Alexis' boss was now dressed as a construction worker. He guessed he was working through a Village People theme as, when he arrived, he was sporting a Native American headdress.

Harry had been briefed by his boss that it would be best not to comment on it. "I made the mistake of laughing at the Heidi costume and it didn't go down well," said Jeffries earlier in the day.

Harry opened the large manila file he had brought with him and started working down the list.

"So far, I have confirmation of the following: All entrances, stairways, elevators and service areas are guarded by Homeland Security agents. SWAT teams will arrive at any moment and take up positions on surrounding buildings. We also have a warrant for the subject's arrest which is mainly for legal reasons, so there is no blowback in the event of us having to use extreme force."

"Good," said the American President, "what about blocking the broadcast signal from the studio in the event they make it through?"

Jacobs looked back at the file and flipped to the next page. "The FBI has a team working on it and they believe it may be possible to kill the transmission in time. In the event that they fail, we have secured confirmation from the owner of the network that Cardinal Johnson will be able to confront the target live on air. He is there now."

"Harry, you idiot," shouted his boss, swinging his arm towards his subordinate. A small rubber duck with a dunces hat flew across the room and bounced off the younger man's forehead before it landed in his coffee. "Stopping that transmission is critical. At the moment, we control the optics of the situation. The last thing we need is this person having a platform to engage with people around the world, even if the Cardinal can refute his claims."

Goncharov tapped the table with the police baton that had appeared along with the rest of the officer's outfit he was now wearing. "Perhaps you should think of a backup plan. Alexi has arranged for a national power outage if the broadcast goes ahead. We already have the emergency broadcast system primed to announce an attack, believed to originate with the alien, currently collaborating with the decadent West against the Russian people."

Lebedev controlled the smug expression on his face but not before Harry had spotted it. "At least this time he has not arranged to blow up an entire tower block while managing to completely miss the targets, only killing one security guard and two pelicans roosting on the roof."

Alexi opened his mouth to respond, but Jeffries interrupted. "Gentlemen, you are both doing a fine job; now, rather than worry about scoring points, let's just make certain our combined resources provide a satisfying outcome for all. Do you have anything else, Harry?"

Jacobs flipped another page. "Actually, yes, I do, Sir. We have had a team of strategists from the CIA working on an analysis of the individual's abilities. Although they believe he does possess significant talents, he does seem to have a blindspot. When the building in Miami was pointlessly blown up," he said, pausing long enough to wink at Alexi, who folded his arms in disgust. "he was unable to see the threat until the last millisecond, hence the casualties in his group."

Goncharov slapped his fist into the baseball mitt he was now wearing as part of his major league outfit. Harry guessed the plague of fancy dress outfits God had visited on him was moving onto a sporting theme. As if to confirm his suspicions, Goncharov's voice became muffled as a Formula 1 racing drivers helmet appeared on his head. He flipped up the visor and continued. "So we are saying larger explosions could catch him out?"

Harry quickly shook his head before the suggestion of a missile strike made it onto the table. "No, but they believe the more things going on around him and the faster the attack, something around a microsecond, could deliver a fatal blow."

"Do we have anything like that in The Black Op's Skunkworks?"

Jacobs pulled out three pictures and passed them around the table. All showed the same photograph. "They believe this may well do the trick."

Each man studied their copy for several seconds before Jeffries spoke. "So it looks like we have a plan. All we need is someone to use it who is expendable in the event anything goes wrong."

Lebedev reached into a briefcase sitting on the chair beside him. We have been tracking this individual for the past few days," Alexi handed a small bio and photo to the others. "He seems to be connected to the girl somehow. Based on our intel, he has a motive to want our target eliminated. His private jet will be touching down at JFK in thirty minutes."

"Can we get him the equipment in time?"

"Yes, Mr President, his accomplice is known to us and has bought weapons from some of our sources. It would be easy to make a phone call and offer him something special to complete his task."

Goncharov nodded his approval.

Jeffries stared at the duck in his hand. It was wearing a red soccer shirt. "With a little luck, our problem will be gone by this time tomorrow."

He flicked the yellow toy into the air over the table as Goncharov jumped to his feet. The President was wearing a tiny white tennis skirt and smashed the duck flat with his newly acquired racket.

***

Once the advert for the televised interview broke, Jeremiah had been lost in his own thoughts. How was he going to compete with this sort of biblical sized media exposure?

The news segment finished on the TV in front of him and it cut to the adverts. Sarah Golding's face appeared, filling the screen. Before the voiceover could start, Jeremiah had pulled out a silver-handled revolver and blown a hole in her forehead. He was surprised that the broadcast continued, even with the cracked screen. He shot it another three times before it decided it was on a losing battle with a .44, fell off the wall and blew up.

An hour later, he had picked up the phone and given instructions to book the flight to New York. Now, on the final approach, Charlie Denis sat opposite him, waiting for instructions. The evangelist had hardly said a word since they took off from Miami. They had now been in silence for thirty minutes. His phone rang and he was grateful for the diversion. 'Number withheld', it said on the screen. In Charlie's line of work, it was far more unusual to see a number come up.

"Yeah?" he said when he accepted the call. Charlie believed brevity sounded more menacing than a wordy monologue. "You have what? How did you get one of those? And it's available? Powerful? No way, that's science fiction. Ok, if you can guarantee it? No, I know you don't give receipts. How much? Christ! Listen, I didn't say no." He looked up at Jeremiah and put his hand over the phone. "How much do you want this guy gone, boss?"

The evangelist looked up with dark sunken eyes.

"What do you mean by 'how much'"

"Half a million dollars, that much."

Jeremiah thought for a moment. That's a good weekend's work, but unless this problem went away and fast, there might not be any more weekends. He nodded.

Charlie removed his hand and spoke to the caller again. "We'll take one. Our plane will be landing in ten minutes. It's at the airport waiting for us? How did you know? Ok, I won't ask. What about payment? You will take an IOU? Are you feeling, ok? Yes, fine by me, see you soon."

He hit 'end', and the phone fell silent, so did Charlie. No one in the underground world he lived in ever gave credit because there was no guarantee the recipient would be alive to pay tomorrow. Something was up.

In the airport car park, the door of the grey van opened and a man climbed out and approached a fully blacked-out limousine that was missing its number plate. A window dropped an inch. "Well?" said Harry Jacobs from the rear seat.

"He agreed, but he was a bit suspicious when I said I didn't need immediate payment."

"Do not worry. The reports on this guy tell me his elevator does not make it to the penthouse. He will be happy with our little toy if it helps him achieve his objective."

The car's trunk opened automatically, and the van driver lifted out a small envelope and a large suitcase. As soon as he closed it, he walked past the window and back to the van.

Alexi sat opposite Jacobs. "Can we trust this courier?"

"I thought you might tidy that loose end up for us when he has made the delivery."

Lebedev nodded, typed the van's license plate into a secure message app on his phone and hit send. "This loose end will be trimmed immediately," he said, as the limo made its way out of the carpark and onto the road back to the city.

***

Caroline came round in Sarah's arms. "Hello baby," she said and leant down to kiss her. "God sends his regards. How are you feeling now?"

"What, after you scared the living daylights out of me by magically appearing out of thin air on the seat next to me? Yeah, good thanks, although I need to check if I should change my underwear."

"I'll check it later for you," said Sarah, helping Caroline sit up.

The two women enjoyed a moment of silence as they sat holding hands. "It's great to see you again," they said in unison and laughed.

Caroline was the first to move things in a business direction. "So is everything ok for the interview, or have we both committed career suicide?"

"I think it is. I spent the morning with him and his friends and he seems the real deal."

"What is he? Angry God from the old testament or God of love from the New Testament and the other religions?"

"I think he is most of the latter. I asked him what parts of each religion were accurate and he wouldn't answer because he didn't want to create a situation where only one section of the people listened to his message. He wants everyone on the planet to hear what he has to say. Apparently, it's vital."

"So, what is it?"

"Again, he wouldn't tell me ahead of time. God believes everyone should hear at the same moment."

Caroline looked concerned, "Are you certain we can trust him? There are some really damning reports coming out of the security agencies around the world."

"I think there are a lot of anxious people in positions of power who have every reason to do all they can to discredit him. They killed one of his friends."

Caroline paused for a moment and then picked up her phone to dial the studio. "Hi, it's me. I want security in the building doubled. No expense spared. What do you mean there is security everywhere? Homeland Security? Ok, thanks." She put the phone in her lap. "We have another problem. The building is full of government agents. There is no way he will get in."

"I wouldn't worry about that; given the shock he gave you, he will make it. I am more concerned about what will happen when he does. How many people will we be broadcasting to?"

The older woman pointed to the picture on the wall. It was a backlit map of the world showing daylight and nighttime zones moving slowly across the surface. Sarah stepped towards it. "Ok, which part?"

"I didn't mean a part of it, Sarah; I meant all of it. This is the biggest story in history. We are being broadcast around the whole planet in real-time."

Sarah turned around, leant back against the wall and slowly slid to the floor.

Caroline walked over, grabbed Sarah's hands and pulled her to her feet. "I know you can do this," she said, cradling the reporters face in her palms, "but if I could ask you a couple of favours?"

"Yes, anything."

"Don't get us fired and don't get us killed. I have some nice plans for our future as long as we have one."

They hugged, and Sarah put her lips close to Caroline's ear. "Don't worry, I've got this," she said.

She just wished she believed what she was saying.

***

Cardinal Johnson had been avoiding contact with people for two hours. After he arrived at the building, to be ushered to a waiting room next to the studio, he had only seen two individuals. One was a security chief from the American service, making sure he was who he said he was, and the second a production assistant called Nick, who was tasked with keeping Johnson fed and watered. The thin young man had asked if there was anything the Cardinal wanted. "Coffee, please," and Nick scurried away to find one. On his return, the assistant made the mistake of handing it directly to the old man. Their fingers touched briefly as the beverage was exchanged, and Johnson immediately leapt back. Since meeting God, he had been cursed with extreme empathic powers. After even the slightest contact of skin meant he saw every event, emotion, and pain a person had felt.

"Are you ok, sir?" said the skinny man picking up the spilt cup.

"Yes, yes, I'm am completely ok." But he wasn't. He wasn't even slightly ok.

"I'll get you another," said the assistant, heading running through the door.

The Cardinal watched him leave and knew Nick would not survive the month. In his mind, he could see all the uncertainty, self-doubt and depression that was swallowing the man's spirit. Johnson knew there would be an empty box of pills lying next to Nick's bed by the time the Cardinal was back in Rome.

"This is not a Christian God," he said out loud. "Christ would never saddle a man with such a terrible curse." Johnson rubbed his hand where they had touched as if he was trying to erase a stain.

"The world must see this imposter for what he is and then we can go back to relying on faith alone. It was much easier praying to a mystical deity than dealing with this real-world God."

NINETEEN

Caroline and Sarah watched the News Network building grow in the window as the limo they were travelling in crept closer through the tragic New York afternoon traffic.

"Perhaps we should have asked your friend for a lift," said Caroline, holding Sarah's hand in the back of the car.

"Actually, I am enjoying the slow route," she said, squeezing her friend's hand and pressing her shoulder closer. "Anyway, he is our friend, not just mine. He sent his regards."

"I have been wondering about that. I thought the gay thing was on his list of no-no's. That would include us, I guess, even though we are not guys."

"Funny, I asked the same question and he said he would prefer not to think about all the creatures he had started in our universe, not to mention all of the other ones that existed in parallel timelines, all having sex, all through existence, all the time. He said it made him feel a bit' icky', all those bodily fluids flying around. Not only between species here but on every world that had developed life."

Caroline looked uncertain. "But I thought it was a big deal for him, especially us?"

"Not for him. We are so insignificant in the greater scheme of things we do not even register. In his words, we are 'Just a tiny blue grain of sand in a desert of stars'. For Bill, it was just the thought of all the sex happening every second, of every day, everywhere where lifeforms had evolved. I guess procreation on that scale is overwhelming when you can see it happening in real-time. In fact, he is amazed we had time to develop a civilisation at all given the amount of time we spent on sex. Bill said he had mentioned it once to someone on our planet a long time ago and, when he came back to visit a thousand years later, every religion was fixated on it. Really, he doesn't care about what we do; he cares about why we do it. He knows it's not our behaviour that is important, it's the intent behind it. Are we adding to the good or subtracting from it?"

Caroline thought about it for a moment. "He sounds like a big-hearted person."

"Except he is not a person; he is The One. He started the universe. Mark, one of the group travelling with him, said he saw it. No, that's not right; he helped him start it by pressing the big red button."

"Mark? Is this your man friend?" Caroline let go of Sarah's hand.

"No, I mean yes, he was, but no, he's not now. Mark has a new girlfriend, and I can only think of you. As soon as we spoke, I knew what I wanted." She caught Caroline by the cheek. "Only you." They kissed and watched as the crowd outside the building slowly enveloped the car.

As they pulled up to the main gate, Caroline pressed the button beside her. "Julie," Caroline said on the car's intercom, "can we park underground and use the service elevator?"

A tinny voice on the speaker said, "No problems Caroline," and the driver swung her car into the tunnel leading to the basement car park. As they pulled up to the door, the car stopped and, before they could get up, Julie had jumped out of the driver's seat and opened the nearside door.

Caroline looked offended as she climbed out. "Julie, I have told you a thousand times; you do not need to open the door for me."

Julie nodded and held the door open. "And I have told you a thousand times that I do not give a rat's ass what you think. You are the only person I have worked for that treated me as a real person, so I will continue to open the door out as a mark of respect, not duty."

"Thank you," said Caroline, "but I will fire you if you keep doing this."

The reprimand would have been impressive if she hadn't been grinning and patting her driver on the shoulder.

Sarah climbed out the same side. "Is she really that nice all the time?" she said in a quiet offstage comment to Julie.

"Miss, I would marry her tomorrow if I could, and I already have a husband and three children. In a world of assholes, she if the sun that shines out of them."

"God likes her," said Sarah.

"And so he should Miss if he is any judge of character."

Julie closed the door and sat back in the driver's seat. She had seen Caroline in a good mood before but never when she had looked so happy. "It looks like life is really working out for you," she said to herself and re-tuned the radio to a local gospel network as she poured herself a coffee from her flask.

"And I say," screeched the preacher on the radio, "this false God is trying to steal your faith! In Romans 1:25 The Bible says, 'they exchanged the truth about God for a lie and worshipped and served the creature rather than the Creator'. Our creator, the one God, has sent this imposter as a test. Look to your hearts where his words have been written on you from birth. If we are to fight this Golden Calf, we must have gold of our own. Phone now to pledge your gold to fight this servant of the devil!" A voiceover person took over as the crescendo finished and, in a more subdued tone, it said. "God's Good Cause Church of the Evangelicals also takes all major credit cards as well as Pay-pall and Bitcoin."

Julie reached for her purse and slipped out a credit card. "Blessed is the one who trusts in the Lord, who does not turn aside to false gods Psalm 40:3-5," she said out loud and dialled the number being read out on the radio, "With God's help, we will mobilise the faithful against this devil," it finished.

When the number was answered, she was immediately connected to a nice lady who managed to up-sell her from a $10 donation to $50 in the following two minutes.

"God bless you," said the voice on the other end of the phone, "this seed you have planted will guarantee you a seat at God's table," and then the line went dead. Julie sat in silence.

For a long time, she thought about the words her father had said to her just before her eleventh birthday and only two days before he died. She had read an advert in a comic that offered a money-back guarantee on every order. It was printed next to a pair of X-ray glasses.

"Julie sweetheart, there are only three things guaranteed in life. Taxes, death and one good moment you remember forever. Anyone else that guarantees you more is selling snake oil."

She sat and thought about his words. After five minutes, she picked up her credit card and turned it over. On the back, it had a magnetic strip with her signature next to a CV code. She turned on the interior light. At the bottom of the piece of plastic, in tiny print that was barely readable, it said 'In case of fraud, contact us on this number'.

She punched the digits into her phone. The call was answered after the first ring. "Fraud line," said the voice, "how can we help?"

Julie hesitated for a moment and then said, "I believe I have made a payment to a fraudulent organisation. I would like to cancel it."

"Certainly, how were you alerted to the fraud?"

"My daddy told me."

"And when did 'your daddy' alert you to this?"

Julie slowly worked out the dates. "Seventeen years, five months and 26 days ago."

The line fell silent for several seconds. "This seems to be a very long time before we have been alerted to the crime. It will fall outside our cancellation policy."

"But I only made the payment a few minutes ago," said Julie.

The line fell silent again. Eventually, the voice said, "I can reverse the transaction for now, but your reason that a voice from your distant past contacted you may mean we have to honour it at a later date."

"It's ok, don't worry about the future. I am guessing they will have run out of snake oil to sell by then," and she hung up the call.

***

It took twenty minutes for Caroline to get to her office. On each corner, corridor and elevator, she had to show her I.D. Both women had been frisked a dozen times. In addition, Sarah had been felt up at least once and threatened with detention twice.

As they finally closed the door, they both sat in the chairs placed on the side of the room. "What the hell was that?" said Sarah. "I thought we were still in America, 'the land of the free and the home of the brave'. Not the bunker of the Gestapo. Did somebody draw a line through the first amendment while I was in Key West?"

Caroline thought about it for a moment. "It's not the land of the free."

Sarah leaned forward. "What do you mean? This is still our home. 'We the people...' and all that."

"They have designated this as an alien terror attack. Emergency powers have come into force. Basically, they can do more or less what they like if it is designated as a terror attack."

"But this is not a terror attack, it's God! How can the government switch from evangelical, bible thumping, mostly Christian, to declaring war on the big guy?"

"Sarah, I love you to bits, but you have to recognise that no open atheist has ever been elected President, and no future Governors ever will. They all visit church before an election, but the statistics tell us that at least half of them do not believe, and many of them break commandments regularly. It's not about the religion; for most of them, it's about the votes they can secure if they pretend they believe."

The two women watched as four agents dressed in black walked past the window, escorting a small man wearing handcuffs and a boiler suit.

"Is that him?" said Caroline.

"No, he tends to wear soccer shirts."

The door opened, and the CEO of the network walked into the room. Terrance was a tall guy with huge shoulders and fifty thousand dollars of dental work shining between his lips. "Good evening! Glad to welcome you onboard, Sarah. Caroline has worn out my ears, telling me how great you are."

'If he only knew what Caroline thought she was really great at,' she thought, blushing.

"Now," he said, "we need to get you into makeup; those rosy cheeks will not work on camera. Now, I have a fabulous addition to the interview tonight." He stepped to one side, and Cardinal Johnson loomed into view.

"I thought it would be better if we had a balanced discussion and that the established church could voice their thoughts."

"A church," said Caroline, frowning.

Terrance looked confused. "A church?"

Caroline walked towards him. "Yes, there are lots of churches and many religions. Why is he the only church chosen?"

"Caroline, this America, we only really have Christian religions, and Cardinal Johnson has kindly flown from Rome to assist us."

She stepped closer and lowered her voice. "Terrance, we are a secular nation. We separate religion and state. This should just be handled by Sarah."

Terrance stepped even closer and leant down to her shoulder. "Caroline, we can separate the state from religion right up until the state wants to charge us with assisting terrorist propaganda. Right now, we are lucky to be planning to air the program."

"This isn't about terrorism vs the first amendment and the freedom of the press. It is about being in someone's pocket. Keep the jumped-up vicar out of our way before this blows up in your face." She stepped back and stood alongside Sarah.

Terrance walked back to the door and put his hand on Johnson's shoulder. "My colleagues will afford you every courtesy Cardinal, and we look forward to seeing you on the show." He walked out, leaving the other man standing in the doorway. As he started to turn, he stopped. "You know this god is not who you think he is. Do not be fooled into believing his lies," he said and closed the door behind him.

Caroline looked concerned.

Sarah held her hand. "Bill is a good guy. Don't worry. Let's get to work on the final questions." She pulled out her notepad and sat down.

Caroline watched as the Cardinal walked along the office's glass wall. He stared at her until he disappeared out of view.

"Ready?" said Sarah.

"Yes," said Caroline, "I think so," and sat down.

TWENTY

At the hotel, Mark was woken by the sound of several trumpets being blown outside the window of Rebecca's thirty-second storey room. He staggered out of bed in the darkness, grabbed the first thing he could find to cover himself and walked over to the window. As he made it to the wall, he pressed the button for the automatic curtains. They pulled apart, but the sky was blotted out by the wings of a group of angels all blowing large silver instruments. As soon as he came into view, they stopped blowing and burst out laughing.

Mark realised he was holding Rebecca's red dress in front of him, and it looked like he was going for a fitting.

"What is it?" said Rebecca.

"Bill has ordered a group of flying comedians to give us an alarm call."

"Are there seven?"

Mark quickly counted them as they headed to the next window to wake up Arsalan.

"Yes, seven angels with trumpets, how did you know?"

"You really should read a bible sometime honey, it's from the Book of Revelation. They blow their trumpets to cue apocalyptic disasters."

"Nice touch," said Mark. "Makes me feel confident about the way the evening will go." He walked back to the bed and dropped Rebecca's dress on the side.

Before it landed, it vanished and re-appeared on a rail hanging next to the bathroom. The material looked like the first time he saw it in the shop window.
"Bill really likes you in that dress."
"It wasn't Bill. I did it. I want to look nice on TV, and also I chose it the first time you met me, so it has sentimental value."
Mark walked over to the dress and then turned back to where he dropped it. "You can manipulate things like Bill? Your powers seem to be changing."
Rebecca stared at the ceiling. She closed her eyes and imagined herself in the dress. When she opened her eyes, she was standing beside Mark with the red silk billowing around her waist. The dress slowly settled into place, and her hair straightened to her shoulders. Although she did not need it, her eyelids darkened, and the lashes lengthened and grew black.
Rebecca caught her reflection in the full-sized mirror across the room as red stilettos appeared on her feet. Her eyes changed colour, and her hair dropped to her waist in golden curls.
"Er, Rebecca, I don't think…" Mark started. Suddenly he grew four inches, and his muscles pumped up like a bodybuilder. He looked in the mirror and watched as his jaw grew squarer just a second before it covered over with a neatly trimmed lumberjacks beard. "…Rebecca, stop."
It was like he had shaken her. In an instant, he was back to normal, and so was she.
"Rebecca…" he said, holding her hand, "…I like you the way you are. We do not need anything superficial. The dress is ok but why would I want to look into different eyes than the ones I fell in love with?"
After her father had died, she had prayed for another man that cherished her just the way she was. Someone

that did not need to change her. Adapt her. Manipulate her.

"I'm sorry. This is too much. How can I control something this big? I'm just a plain girl from a poor home." She looked up at Mark. He no longer resembled Atlas holding the world on his shoulders. Now he was just the tall, trustworthy, kind man dressed as an 80's cowboy throwback. "Can I at least get rid of those?" she said, looking down.

He stared at the western boots he was wearing. The Cuban heels were worn, and the patina was dull. "You may refresh them but not replace them."

Immediately they began to shine and recovered their youth.

"Better," she said.

"Perfect," he replied. "Now, we need a shower so we can meet up with the rest."

"We should hurry; they will be waiting. We could save time by showering together." She took Mark's hand and lead him to the bathroom.

"You, young lady, are a bad influence. What would your grandparents think?"

"Up until a few days ago, your mother was happy to think my ancestor got a young virgin pregnant, perhaps without explicit consent. I think us showering together is mild in comparison. Don't you?"

"For God's sake, don't mention that to mom. Bill will never hear the last of it."

They stepped into the shower and an hour later fell into the hall giggling.

Marion leant against a wall with her arms folded. "You just can't control yourself, can you, Mark?"

He threw his hands in the air. "Mom, it's not my fault; it's Bill's granddaughter. She is a bad influence."

Marion walked over, slapped her son on the shoulder and headed for the lift.

Rebecca punched him gently in the ribs. "Wow, how quickly you threw me under your mom's bus-of-morals when things got tough. You will have to pay penance for that later." And she playfully dug her fingernails into his ribs.

Marion passed Bill and shot him a loaded glance. "I blame you. Your morals are not what I was lead to believe from the good book."

Mark followed her, smiling. "Yes mom, you should have realised that when he started chasing young virgins."

Rebecca punched him even harder in his back as Marion shuddered to a halt. She turned back to Bill with a scowl on her face. "Well?" she said.

Bill held his hands out, waving them to indicate the negative. "I keep telling you. Two thousand-year-old books written by mostly unknown people are not the most reliable source of information. I was there, and I can tell you that was not the case. Who do you want to believe? Me, God, the person on the ground at the time it happened, or a bunch of people who copied stories from other, more ancient cultures in part one. And then, in part two, embellished the life of a really nice young man who came to an untimely end?"

The hall fell silent. No one wanted to comment.

"Good." said Bill. "Sometimes, it feels like you are all happier to believe an old storybook than the actual God it is based on."

He snapped his fingers, and they all disappeared.

***

Caroline stood behind one of the studio cameras and watched a makeup artist touching up Sarah's lipstick as she sat in the interviewer's chair underneath the spotlights. In her ear, voices from the control both were shouting in a mild panic. It was thirty seconds to air time, and the clock on the wall was relentlessly ticking them away.

She walked over to Sarah and mouthed the words, "Where the hell are they?"

Sarah shrugged.

Loud enough to be heard, she asked what she should do.

"Go live on time," said Sarah, "that's all we can do. I trust Bill. He will be here."

Outside the main studio doors, four agents waited quietly, staring at the elevator doors halfway down the corridor. With fifteen seconds to go, the bell sounded to announce an arrival. All four operatives drew their guns and stepped forward as the doors opened.

The production assisted stepped into the hall and immediately jumped back in again as he saw the barrels of the pistols pointing at him. Before the doors could close again, all four agents were crowded into the elevator, pinning the poor man to the wall. "Who are you and why are you here?" growled the man, holding his wrists behind his back.

"My name is Nick; I work here."

One of the men picked up the box that the young man had been carrying. "What's in here?"

"Doughnuts, some guy called Bill told me to get some for you to eat while you were waiting for the interview to finish."

They looked at each other and then sprinted back to the door. It was locked tight. One agent stepped back and fired at the catch. As the hammer dropped, the gun fell to pieces and clunked to the floor.

The others levelled their weapons and pulled the triggers.

Now there was a considerable pile of gun parts at their feet.

Nick caught up with the group. "Do you still want the doughnuts?" he said, opening the box and helping himself to a plump one with pink icing.

Inside the studio, Sarah was sitting in front of four cameras. One red 'recording' light had just flashed on. For a second, she froze as its glass face stared coldly at her. And then she began.

"Tonight will be one of the most eagerly awaited events of the last two thousand years. If tonight's guest claims are true, we will be talking to God, the creator of the universe and the person who spawned many religions throughout mankind's history. I have spoken to him and he assures me he has returned with a message for every person on the planet."

She paused and glanced towards the clock. Bill was over a minute late. Sarah started to panic and opened her mouth to fill more time when a loud pop filled the studio and Bill, Marion, Rebecca, Mark, and Arsalan appeared next to her. Millie popped into existence on Sarah's lap and immediately started licking the presenter's hand.

A couple of the crew gasped, and the voices in Caroline's ear started shouting louder.

After breathing a sigh of relief, Sarah motioned for them to take a seat in the chairs waiting for them on stage.

Outside the studio, mobile phones started ringing in the agents' pockets. The commander answered when he saw who was calling.

"No, sir, they did not get past us. We have been right outside the door. No sir, we have not been asleep. The doors are locked from the inside. No, sir, we have tried that. The guns keep falling to pieces, all of them. Yes, we did, and they fell apart again. The noise? We are using axes to break down the door. No sir, they keep falling to pieces too." The phone went dead.

"I believe the President is a little upset," said the commander.

"What now?" said one of the agents, putting his gun together for the fifth time. As soon as it was finished, he cocked it and it fell onto the floor in pieces.

"Now, ladies and gentlemen, I suggest we have a doughnut unless any of you geniuses can think of another idea."

The other three shrugged and helped themselves to the cake.

Back inside the studio, the lights flickered for a moment and then steadied. Sarah looked concerned, but Bill reassured her.

"It is ok; someone just tried to turn off the power to the building to stop your interview. I turned it back on."

Sarah nodded, regained her composure and looked down at her list of questions. "So God, if I may call you that, can I just confirm that you are The God and not an alien interloper as has been stated by some of the world's media?

"Yes, I am God, but I would prefer you to call me Bill; it is less formal."

Mark opened his mouth to explain, but Bill mouthed the words, "not now."

"It's good to meet you again, Sarah," he turned and waved at the person standing open-mouthed next to one of the cameras. "Hi Caroline," he said, smiling.

"Nice to meet you. These are my friends; Arsalan, who is visiting from abroad, Rebecca, and this is Mark and Marion Schneider."

Caroline waved hello.

Sarah watched the interchange and thought she needed to get back in control. Maybe some polite small talk would bring her back into the conversation. "Marion, I used to know a family called Schneider. Are you related to one of the Long Island Schneiders?"

Marion folded her arms. "No, my father was one of the 'let's get the hell out of Europe before a nazi blows our brains out' Schneiders."

Sarah looked from her to Mark and thought she had had a lucky escape; Marion could have been her mother in law. She turned back to Bill.

"God… …I mean, Bill, there are a lot of people watching this program who will be very sceptical about your claim to be God, the creator of our universe."

"He definitely is," Mark chipped in, nervously staring at the camera. Although he spent his life on YouTube presenting The Godless Experience, a small internet phone-in show was a lot different from addressing billions of people worldwide. "In fact, I was there. I watched him do it; in fact, I pressed…"

Bill shook his head and whispered, "Not helping," in Marks's ear.

"Perhaps a little miracle will help people believe me," said Bill.

"Great," said Sarah, "as long as it's not a global flood." She laughed at her own joke but was the only one who did.

"Just to be clear. I didn't flood the planet last time. It was a little river in Egypt that I made burst its banks to irrigate some crops and I was just trying to be helpful."

"But what about The Ark?"

"Don't get me started on that. All I said was that the man standing on the bank should put his two goats in the boat to save them from drowning. Three thousand years later, I'm the bad guy and get the blame for murdering nearly all the life on the Earth. And people wonder why I don't get involved with the day to day affairs of your planet. I never get any thanks."

Sarah realised she was losing control again. "Perhaps you have another idea?"

Bill thought for a moment. He snapped his fingers and everybody in the room was suddenly wearing their local team's soccer shirt. As a treat, they were all holding a glass of milk and a box of popcorn. Outside the studio, the four agents were each sporting USA National Soccer shirts. One of them looked out the window. The people down on the street were wearing all different types too.

"Everyone on the planet has exactly the same," said Bill.

Rebecca leant over, "Could I have a beer instead? I am lactose intolerant?"

"What? said, Bill.

"About 68% of the world's population are lactose intolerant."

"Oh great, in a thousand years, this will be known as The Great Milk Plague sent by God. Ok, how about this?" He snapped his fingers, and everyone's drink turned into their personal favourite. "Better?"

Sarah took a sip out of her glass of Champagne.

"Much, now can we get back on course. Why have you returned after so many years?"

Bill looked straight down the lens of the camera. "I have visited Earth many times in its history and tried to steer evolution in the right direction, and each time things worked out ok."

"Apart from the dinosaurs," said Arsalan, "you did make a mess of that. I mean, great for us but not so great for them."

Bill glared at him.

Arsalan took a sip of his beer. "Sorry, but just saying, you know, it wasn't a perfect result, but then again, no one's perfect, I suppose."

Bill wondered if it was too late to go back and divert the asteroid that killed them off. No, he guessed he was stuck with the monkeys.

"This time," he continued, "I have to leave it up to you to save your species. In each universe, every life-form finally reaches a turning point in their evolution where they can adapt and continue, or carry on as before and fail to survive. This moment is yours."

"Are you saying this 'the end of days', as foretold by the Bible? Armageddon?" asked Sarah.

"Listen, I have been banging on about this since you managed to develop language skills 150,000 years ago. Why do you think most religions incorporate a story that describes an apocalyptic end to the world?"

A new voice, hidden in the shadows, echoed across the room. "The true Lord God would be applauding the arrival of the end times," Cardinal Johnson strode onto the stage wearing a Fiorentina soccer shirt.

"Nice touch," thought Mark, remembering that the team had been caught in a match-fixing scandal a few years earlier.

Johnson stepped in front of the cameras. "Our almighty father has promised that, at the end of our world, we will enjoy the rapture and join our true God in heaven while all non-believers will meet their fate in hell. Why would the real God warn us about the coming of judgement day when true believers will welcome it?"

"Just one problem, the heaven thing," said Rebecca, "apparently it's not what you were lead to believe. Like not at all, and as for hell, that's not on the cards for anyone, regardless of your belief. Hey, look, I'm disappointed too, but we are where we are," she shrugged.

The Cardinal's voice rose, "This is proof to all people of religion. Only an imposter god would lie about our chances of resurrection. The real God promised us eternity in paradise, and no Devil with a pocketful of tricks will make us worship a false god. You are blasphemy in a soccer shirt and no god of ours!" He stormed off the stage.

"Look," said Bill, rising to his feet, "I understand that the heaven thing may come as a shock to many people."

"Not me," said Mark, "I never believed in one anyway."

Both Marion and Rebecca hit him at the same time.

"Anyway," said Bill, trying to continue, "your race has become an infestation on the planet. You are ruining your own world and, if you do not change your ways, the Earth will fight back. It cannot sustain you if you destroy its ecosystem. If mankind does not take immediate action, you have little more than a generation left before it is too late."

The room fell silent for several seconds.

"But if you are God, you could just snap your fingers and fix it," said Sarah. "Why wouldn't you help us?"

Sarah, "While we have been talking, five other developed race have become extinct through natural disasters or actions of their own. I like mankind; that's why I'm here, but at some time, every parent must let their child find its own way in life, and this is yours."

Marion placed her hand on Bill's shoulder as he sat down. "How can we change? What should we do?"

"Do what you know is right. Follow the golden rule. It is the only one I ever suggested you stick to."

"What is that?" said Sarah.

"Treat others as you want to be treated. If you do that and stop standing on the heads of the other sheep to get ahead, you will work it out. Now is the time to dispense with tribal factions, local governments and exclusive religions. You have the chance to be one people working together to save yourselves, not just to advance your own self-interests. Good luck," he said and snapped his fingers. The small group disappeared, along with Sarah and Caroline.

Immediately the door burst open and the room filled with gun-toting SWAT officers, each one shouting for people to get on the ground. No one moved; they just stood transfixed, staring at the empty chairs.

Eventually, the officers stopped shouting because no one was taking any notice. As soon as they did, a doughnut and coffee appeared in each person's hands, replacing the guns that had vanished.

TWENTY ONE

In the Whitehouse situation room, Goncharov was still screaming into the phone in Russian. Eventually, he threw it at the wall.

"Not good news?" said Jeffries. He was surrounded by rubber ducks dressed in black suits and sunglasses that had appeared when he was shouting at the agents stationed at the studio.

"My incompetent generals in Moscow failed to trigger the power cut. Every television switched to the emergency broadcast channel which suddenly started playing the interview."

"At least most of them will not have understood it; the broadcast was in English."

"Apparently not. My generals assure me God and the others were all speaking Russian!"

Jeffries thought about it for a moment. "That would make sense. A message for the world, broadcast in every language on the planet."

Goncharov tried to sit down, but the giant dragons tail attached to the costume he was wearing made it virtually impossible. "What now?"

"Now my friend, we start the machine working. I have instructed every pro-government commentator to take to the airwaves on radio, television and social media. I assume you will do the same."

"It is already in hand. We have a whole disinformation division working and, by morning, these people will be either dead or unable to stand against the overwhelming public reaction we will generate." Goncharov's tail disappeared, and a golden horn appeared on his forehead. The rest of his body was wrapped in a unicorn outfit but with only two legs. He noticed the tail had vanished, so he sat down.

"Must be mythical animals hour," thought Jeffries and started chewing the beak of the bank robber duck he was now holding. "I am declaring a state of national emergency and mobilising the National Guard. We have to find them before they can do any more damage."

His phone rang. "Hello."

"Good evening, sir, it's Harry Jacobs. I am outside the target's hotel with Mr Lebedev."

"How nice, enjoying New York are you? It looked like a nice evening WHEN YOU TWO FAILED TO STOP A SIMPLE T.V. PROGRAM!"

Harry waited a few seconds before putting the phone back to his ear. Mr President, we believe them to be inside. What would you like us to do?"

"I think you should make them a round of sandwiches and brew a pot of tea. What do you mean what do we want you to do, KILL THEM YOU IDIOT!"

Alexi heard the other half of the conversation, even without it being on speakerphone. He watched out of the window as his operative from Miami pulled up across the street in a van. H had called his agent earlier to give him the address. The big guy grabbed a rucksack and climbed out. Without locking the vehicle's door, he ran into the foyer and turned towards the elevators. "It looks like I did make the correct call. Now we wait."

**

210

Charley had been trying to put together the contents of the briefcase he and Jeremiah had purchased from the arms dealer at the airport. It had taken nearly thirty minutes, but it looked like everything was in place. The device looked like something out of a sci-fi movie. Measuring three feet long, it looked bulky with a colossal cartridge jammed in the handle. When he flicked on the arming switch, the dangerous end glowed red, and a gentle hum filled the air around them. Charlie looked at a small sticker on the side of the weapon. 'Plasma, extreme care required.'

"No shit." he said to himself.

"So how powerful is it?" said Jeremiah.

"I am not completely sure. These things are not supposed to exist. You know the movie with the aliens killing everyone and people firing giant guns at them? Well, this is one of those guns, except this one is not fiction."

Jeremiah picked it up and stepped onto the hotel balcony. It had taken most of the day, but eventually, he had bribed an executive at the T.V. station to check their system for hotel bookings. Eventually, he got the news he needed. God was booked to stay the night a few blocks away. After another sizeable bribe, he managed to get a room at the other hotel facing directly towards theirs across the small park.

He swung the weapon up and the scope illuminated automatically. In the view finder he could see directly into several of the rooms in their building. After moving back and forth several times, he noticed a room dimly lit but with no one in it.

Suddenly, a small group magically appeared out of thin air and in the middle was God.

Jeremiah couldn't believe his luck. He squeezed the trigger but, just as he was about to fire, God stepped to one side and disappeared behind the rest of the group. He eased the pressure of the trigger. "Patience Jeremiah," he said to himself. "It's not often you get to kill God."

***

"So what now?" said Mark, sitting on Bill's bed next to Rebecca.

"Now we see what happens. I guess we will know if worked by mankind's response over the next twenty-four hours."

Arsalan stepped over to the window and stood next to Marion. She held his hand. "How are you now?" she said.

Arsalan thought about it for a moment. "Not as angry as I was, although I still think it was my fault Paul isn't here." He couldn't quite say the word 'alive'. "I did think about asking Rebecca if there was anything she could do, but the explosion swallowed him. She nearly died saving me; there is no way she could do anything for Paul."

"He saved you; now, all you have to do is work out how you can make something out of his sacrifice." Marion gasped and let go of his hand. She placed both of hers against the glass as she looked down. A flash of fire lit up the street, engulfing a parked car. As they watched, a bottle sailed through the air and hit another, igniting the petrol inside the Molotov Cocktail.

"It has started," Arsalan said. As he looked down, he watched a familiar dark figure walk casually into the building as if he did not even notice the fires. "I need to go for a while," he said and walked out of the room. He headed towards his own suite while taking his phone out of his pocket.

Caroline and Sarah joined Marion at the window. A shopfront shattered and glass fell into the street as a second rock was thrown.

On the bed, Rebecca reached for the remote control and switched on a news channel.

She turned up the sound as pictures of darkened city streets flashed back and forth. "…and as we can see, sporadic looting is breaking out in many cities. In others, groups are marching. Some in support of tonight's broadcast, but most are angry at what social media is calling 'a direct attack on religions around the world'. People are angry, and we are catching up with them to hear what they have to say." The picture changed to an outside broadcast team in Chicago. The reporter was walking alongside the leader of a group of about a hundred people. He was carrying an assault rifle and a placard. It read, "You put your hands on my religion and I'll put mine around your throat!"

"Sir," shouted the reporter of the sound of the crowd, "how do you feel about what God said tonight?"

The man stopped. "He may be your god, but he sure as hell isn't mine. My god will be taking my family and me through the pearly gates when the end of the world really comes and sending those Mormons, Scientologists, Muslims, as well as all those other cranky churches to the fiery pit where they belong. When that time eventually comes, I will be in heaven, throwing coals down to stoke those flames good and high."

"And where are you going now?"

"Right now, we are going to protest until the government does something about this alien devil or whatever he is. I just wish we were in New York so we could find him ourselves. Isn't that right?" he shouted to the crowd, and a massive cheer went up.

The picture switched to a similar scene in what looked like Los Angeles.

"Turn it down," said Caroline, "I know how this will play out. All the media will chase the most radical demonstrations in the hope of capturing more graphic violence to gain viewers. Got to love my industry sometimes. As soon as we started making money out of news programs, news programs started making the news."

"At least there is still the BBC in England. One last bastion of fairness," said Sarah.

Rebecca flicked the channel over and the BBC World News logo appeared. Although there was no sound now, a picture of a reporter chasing a large group of protesters through London's streets appeared, as a mob smashed windows and set fire to cars.

"We are doomed," said Sarah. "Didn't anyone listen to what you said, Bill?"

Bill opened the minibar, which was completely filled with Pabst Blue Ribbon. He pulled one out, cracked the seal and drank it in one go. "Yes they did, Sarah. Although we were not the most impressive media team to ever hit the television, we got the message over, and the audience heard it. The problem was, most people were listening with their fingers in their ears. I had worried about this. Do you know the expression 'monkey trap'? Well, you monkeys are stuck in one."

"What's a monkey trap?" said Marion quietly to Sarah.

"It's normally something like a coconut with a hole in the end which is staked to the ground by a chain at the other. People put small amounts of food in them. When the monkey wanders along, it squeezes its hand in through the hole, grabs the food, which causes it to make a fist. Now it can't get its hand out and the hunters run up a kill it."

"Why doesn't the monkey let go of the food?"

"Value rigidity. The monkey values what it has in its hand and can't let go, even though, to keep hold of it will mean its death."

"Exactly," said Bill, "you monkeys value your place in society and the social groups you have built. To abandon that sets people adrift mentally, and men find it difficult to deal with, so they will desperately try to keep hold of the position they have. 'Better the devil you know' and all that."

Marion shook her head in disbelief. "But they will die. That cannot make sense."

Caroline sat on the end of the bed. "I'm afraid it does to us monkeys."

"Can we stop referring to the human race as monkeys," said Rebecca. "I am certain people will come to their senses."

Bill laughed. "Don't hold your breath. Now people will become emotionally invested in their beliefs. Soon their cognitive bias kicks in."

Marion looked at Sarah with eyebrows raised and a question on her face.

"What Bill is trying to say, Marion, although not in a very straightforward way, is that when people become invested in a belief, they start becoming biased to the information they receive that supports that belief. The brain only hears what it wants to hear, so the Cardinal's message will be what they took away tonight, not ours. Believing his lies means people do not have to change their religion, social hierarchy or behaviour. Why do you think people love a good conspiracy theory, regardless of how crazy it seems. Believing anything is better than destroying everything you have faith in."

"And that, my friends, is why we are now done." Bill got to his feet. "Can I just say it has been a pleasure to meet you all and, if any of you survive the collapse of your world's ecosystem, I will say high to your great-great-grandchildren when I pop by next time."

Mark jumped off the bed. "Bill, are you kidding? You can't leave? We need you."

"Sorry Mark, I have done what I can and it didn't work, but I really liked meeting you. I was right; you are a good man and perfect for Rebecca; it's just a shame you will be dead in twenty years."

Bill strolled past Mark, who was in a state of shock. Rebecca climbed off the bed. "I guess it's a waste of time trying to change your mind."

"Afraid so, I have work to do three universes away. I am glad I had a chance to meet you. Your great great great… …anyway, your grandmother would be very proud." He hugged her, turned, waved good-bye and disappeared.

"Well," said Marion, to quote Winston Churchill, 'I think we are buggered'."

"Did he really say that?" said Mark.

"He went to the boys boarding school at Harrow in about 1888, so yes, he probably did at some time." She picked up one of the beers, opened the top and copied Bill by drinking the contents in one go.

***

In the room a floor beneath Arsalan's, Ayaan unloaded his pistol and checked it over, then reloaded it. With a quick pull on the slide, he chambered the first round. It had been an easy process to gain access to the T.V. company's computer and check for bookings made at local hotels. Luck was on his side. There was only one. His phone rang and he answered.

"Ayaan, we have been monitoring the situation," said a voice he recognised.

In ten years, it had only spoken to him twice. Both times to congratulate him on a job well done. It was not often anyone talked to the Cleric.

"Although you have made good progress, we wish you to stand down."

Ayaan could not believe what he was hearing. "But we must finish this. Our justice demands it."

"I understand how you feel, but things have changed; Arsalan contacted me. He believes this is our God."

"Arsalan is a blasphemer! He is crazy and has been beguiled by this imposter," shouted Ayaan down the phone.

"Yes, that may be the case. Perhaps I am making a mistake trusting him, but he went to great lengths, even putting his life on the line by disclosing his location, to assure me we were wrong and that this person is who he says he is."

Ayaan's head was spinning. He could not believe what he was hearing.

"Stand down, Ayaan. Let us see if this is our God and if we are blessed with his return." The phone clicked as the call was ended.

For several minutes he stared at it as if it was a deadly snake in his hand. Eventually, he threw it to one side. "No." he said and turned back to the table.

He laid the gun to one side so it was resting on top of a long black briefcase. He then unzipped a rucksack that laid next to it. Methodically, he unpacked several bars of Semtex, an electronic trigger and a mobile phone. Within minutes he had constructed a bomb and laid it in the middle of the room. He checked the bag and took out another mobile phone the same as the first and put it in his pocket. He checked the connection one last time and moved to leave. Ayaan was only three feet from the door when he heard a loud hiss. Instantly there was a bang as something metal knocked the door of its hinges. Before he could pull his gun, a large chrome fire extinguisher spraying CO_2 into the air landed on the floor in front of him. The room filled with a cloud of white gas. He managed three shots towards the door before someone tasered him from behind.

Arsalan stood over him as he lay on the floor, convulsing.

"You should have quit while you were ahead, my friend. Now, this is the end of your little rampage." He picked up Ayaan's gun and pointed it at his head.

***

Jeremiah had watched God step into view again and again. He nearly shot when he was drinking a beer and then again as he walked to the bed. When Rebecca had stepped into view, he froze. What was she still doing with them? By the time he recovered his senses, they were hugging. Finally, God stepped into the open, and Jeremiah smiled, "Got you."

God disappeared.

He swung the gun to the other windows but nothing. He had blown it. What was he going to do now?

A movement caught his eye, and he swung the scope back to the other room. Rebecca was walking with a tall man. They opened the door, and then, a few seconds later, the light turned on in another room across the hall.

Rebecca walked into the light, and suddenly, the man was with her. Holding her. Kissing her.

Jeremiah exploded with rage and pulled the trigger.

***

Ayaan came round, sitting in a chair, facing the window. On the table three metres in front of him, Arsalan pointed the gun at Ayaan's head.

"You have been spoken to by the Cleric?"

"I don't know what lies you have told him, but it will not work on me." Ayaan started to move, but Arsalan shook his head. "Even you can not make it to me before I shoot."

Ayaan sat back. "Then I suggest you shoot."

"I have a better idea." Arsalan leant forward and flicked a switch on the top of the bomb. A red light started blinking. He turned on the mobile phone his friend had set up as a trigger. "You blew up a good man the last time you tried to kill me, a religious man.

"You were lucky; you were dying when they magicked you away."

Arsalan opened his shirt. "Yes my friend. I was, and they healed me. Just like in our holy book. Look, I do not even have a scratch."

Ayaan looked at the man's chest. The last time he had seen him laying on the hood of the car, he had a cut in it so deep he could see Arsalan's ribs.

"So, I have only two choices," said Arsalan. "Kill you and break my promise with God or this." He threw the gun onto the floor between them and tossed the detonator into Ayaan's lap.

"I trust you to make the right decision. If I am wrong and blow us up, you will be a martyr and will be accepted in God's grace. If I am right, you will kill your best friend for no reason at all. Your choice."

Ayaan looked at Arsalan, grabbed the gun and dived across the room at the other man.

***

In the next room, the Russian had extracted 10 bars of C4 from out of his rucksack. In a mirror of Ayaan's procedure a few minutes earlier, he placed a detonator on the table and a mobile phone next to it. It took him twice as long to put the parts together but, when it was finished, the device looked double the size and ten times deadlier.

As soon as it was finished, he placed two other phones on the table. One a twin of the item attached to the bomb and the other a brand new smartphone.

He sat and stared at the screen, waiting for a call to arrive, which would give him the go-ahead for his plan. "Try to dodge a blast four meters under your feet." He lay back and put his feet on the table.

TWENTY TWO

As Rebecca stepped into her room, she started to cry. Mark was still a few feet behind her. As he caught up, he put his arms around her. "I know it's disappointing. You have only just found who you are, and now Bill has abandoned you."

"It's not abandoning me, it's abandoning everyone on Earth that hurts." Several storeys below, the streets were filling with screams, shots and the occasional explosion. "I really thought we were going to save the world. How could we fail with God on our side?"

"We are not lost yet." Mark turned her around. "We can still try to make a difference. I want a future for us."

Rebecca reached up and pulled his lips down to hers. "I love you," she said, and before he could tell her the same, she kissed him.

Across the park, a blinding flash lit up Jeremiah's face as he pulled the trigger and a ball of plasma, travelling at Mk 5, streaked over the park. It tore a twenty-foot hole in the wall of their hotel and ripped Mark out of her arms. It threw him in the air and smashed him against the opposite wall.

A second before Jeremiah had shot at the floor above, Aayan had leapt at Arsalan, gun in hand. As the old man collided with his friend, Arsalan was thrown back and pinned against the floor.

"Still!" hissed Ayaan.

He rolled off Arsalan and crawled along the table towards the window. As he passed the briefcase, he grabbed hold of the handle and dragged it with him. Arsalan was still in shock. He had imagined his old friend was going to shoot him and then blow up Bill's room. Now he realised he was not going to die; well, not in the short term. He crawled after Ayaan and, by the time he caught up, his friend had opened the case and assembled a compact sniper rifle. Ayaan raised the stock and pointed it through the large gap in the curtains.

"Ayaan, what is it?"

Instead of answering, he handed the gun to Arsalan and pointed it across the park to a building on the opposite side. As the young man lifted it to his eye, the telescopic sight filled with a picture of the crazed man wildly swinging something that looked like a small, handheld canon with a glowing red end like a cigarette. He handed it back it Ayaan. "What's he doing and what is he holding?"

"He is a T.V. evangelist who we have been following for the last few days and that, in his hand, is a plasma gun. I think he may be about to try and kill God."

As if prompted, the crazy man pulled the trigger, and a bolt of death exploded out of the barrel of the gun. Above them, it slammed into the building and half a ton of masonry fell past their window, heading for the street.

Without thinking, Ayaan's years of training kicked in. He slowed his breathing, exhaled, and squeezed the trigger. Two hundred feet away, a bullet tore through Jeremiah's neck. His body spun 180 degrees and he fell back against the corner of the balcony. A second bullet caught him in the chest, lifting him into the air, rolling him over the railing, and the evangelist started his swift journey to the sidewalk ten storeys below.

As soon as the second shot had left the gun, both men were on their feet, running for the door. Arsalan was through it first with Ayaan on his heels.

At the next door along the corridor, a huge man with blond hair and a gun in his hand jumped out. Over Arsalan's shoulder, a bullet raced past him, caught the other man in the ear and slammed him back into his room. Instantly the door swung closed as if to say 'nothing to see here, move along'.

"Russian hitman," shouted Ayaan, as if that was enough to make sense of the gunfire.

"Stop shooting people," shouted Arsalan. "I promised God."

"I didn't," shouted the other man as they burst through the fire escape door and sprinted up the stairs. "I just incapacitated him."

"You incapacitated him into the afterlife. An afterlife that doesn't exist!"

"Oops," shouted Ayaan, trying to keep up with his friend.

***

Rebecca's ears were ringing. Her shoulder was shattered, and blood was running down the inside of her dress. She staggered to her feet, trying to make sense of the broken room around her. Where the window and the wall had been, the night air blew through uninterrupted.

"Mark!"

In a corner at the back of the suite was a bundle of twisted clothes. Except they were not clothes. Fabric doesn't bleed. She ran over, ignoring the searing pain trying to cripple her movement.

As she fell next to him, the rest of the group ran into the room through the shattered door. Just behind

Marion and the others, Arsalan and Ayaan crowded at their back. Rebecca pointed to the window. "There!" she said, "It's someone there!"

"No, he's not," said Arsalan. "My friend sent him ten storeys to the street."

She dropped to her knees and pushed Mark's body flat. As soon as she reached him, she knew he was dead. As their skin touched, the spark between them was gone.

"No no no no NOOO! Please no...". She started sobbing and fell on his chest. "BILL, YOU GET BACK HERE RIGHT NOW AND FIX THIS!" she screamed.

The room fell silent. Marion stood, ashen-faced with tears tracing lines down her cheeks.

Two minutes later, nothing had changed.

Arsalan sat beside Rebecca. "I am sorry, Rebecca, but we need to leave; there is no way of knowing how many more people are on their way. We need to get you to safety."

"No," she said.

"Yes," said Arsalan. "Look, we need to leave."

"Arsalan," she said, as she pointed to Mark's body, "I meant, no!"

Rebecca put her hands on her boyfriend's chest and breathed out. Everybody started to feel the heat radiating from her body and stepped back. The light began to build until it was impossible to look towards the couple. Parts of the partially destroyed ceiling fell to the floor as the air started to roar.

Sarah shouted over the noise, "Rebecca don't, you cant bring him back- It will kill you. Let him go!"

The light grew so intense it shone through Caroline's eyelids, even though she had closed them and her hands were clutched across her eyes.

Suddenly, there was a violet flash, and each of them gasped as intense heat washed through their bodies. In the car outside, Jacobs and Lebedev watched the sky lit up for a mile in every direction. For five minutes, they had been trying to contact the Russian agent tasked with blowing up the targets, but with no luck.

Harry looked at his Russian counterpart. "Alexi. Have you ever been to Montana?"

"No, isn't a long way from here?"

"Yes, and that may be a good thing. I have always wanted to open a bar there and maybe now would be a good time. Want to join me?"

Alexi thought about the reception he would get from his boss. "Harry my comrade, Montana is calling."

Above them, the hotel room returned to its subdued lighting. Rebecca stood next to Mark. He looked dazed, but he was breathing.

Rebecca leant against his body and held his hand. "See Bill, I did it without you," and she collapsed on the floor. Mark cradled her face. "Rebecca?" He couldn't feel a pulse in her neck.

He realised this war zone was no place for her, so he picked her up and took her back to his unscathed room.

"BILL!" he screamed, as he walked through the door and laid her on the bed. The rest of the group followed him, expecting a small soccer fan to arrive and save his grandchild.

Mark waited.

All at once, a roaring noise filled the room.

Marion turned around. "Thank God."

The room filled with light, and everyone was blinded. Then the roaring became a loud hum, and a tinny voice echoed around the room. "This is the NYPD.

Hello, It's God

Remain in your rooms. There is a civil disturbance
below. For your own safety, remain in your rooms.
The helicopter moved on, and the noise faded.
Mark sat on the bed holding Rebecca's hand.
God was silent.

TWENTY THREE

The mobile phone on the plain wooden table began to ring.

A few bars of Bob Dylan's "Knockin' on Heaven's Door" echoed around the room. Compared to the plain desk, the rest of the chamber was quite luxuriant. On the opposite wall, a painting of the San Francesco al Prato Resurrection by the Italian Renaissance painter Pietro Perugino dominated the room.

A priest, standing beside the mobile, lifted the device to his ear and answered. "This is His Holiness's phone; who may I say is calling?" the Father nodded and handed the phone to The Pope.

"It is his friend, the Cleric."

An arm slipped out of the robe and gently took the phone.

"Pronto," he said, indicating he was ready to talk.

"My friend, I believe we should discuss our matter at hand." The Cleric's voice was clear and definite but very welcoming.

"I agree. What are your thoughts?"

"My thoughts? I believe I am at the stage where I am running out of them. At the moment, I have only one left."

The Pope smiled; he always enjoyed how his counterpart cut straight to the heart of the matter.

"And what thought are you left with?"

"I think we have made a mistake. Both of us were rightly sceptical, but, after a conversation with one of my team who has built a relationship with God... ... Bill, he has convinced me this is the real thing."

"You have more local intel than I do. My man there seems to have lost his grip on reality; accusing er... ...Bill on television was wrong. I understood the Cardinal was only seeking understanding, but now I believe he has unilaterally declared war. He is being repatriated as we speak."

"So where do we go from here?"

"Perhaps we could manage a joint communication. I could meet you in Istanbul in a few hours."

The Cleric thought about it for a moment. "This sounds good, but why Istanbul?"

"It is the geographical meeting point of our two religions. We could also invite other representatives to join us."

"Let us do this; I will make the arrangements and see you soon."

***

Cardinal Johnson waited as his driver slid the key card through the lock on the Miami safe house gate.

He called through the open window. "When we get inside, I want you to organise a meeting with our press secretary, local operations manager and tailor. They should be here in an hour. I need a new propaganda campaign, a couple of agents and a suit for my next television appearance."

The limousine pulled up at the door, which automatically opened just as it had for Father Paul a day before. As his old boss headed for the house, the driver walked to the car's trunk to get the bags.

He looked down at the three huge suitcases. How could the Cardinal need more clothes? He wasn't exactly travelling light. His natural assumption was that Johnson could put clothes on his expenses as a cost to his trip.

As he struggled through the door with the bags, the Cardinal was sitting facing him with silver tape over his mouth.

The driver stopped and dropped the bags.

Four priests dressed in plain black robes were making busy around the Cardinal.

One was cable tying Johnson's legs together, another was doing the same to his wrists. In the distance, the third was opening a large packing crate, and the last pulled out a syringe and filled it from a small phial.

They all stopped and looked at the driver.

"Carry on," he said as he turned around, closed the door and ran to the car.

Johnson started panicking, rocking back and forth, pulling at the ties.

Without slowing, the fourth Father stuck the syringe into the Cardinal's neck. In seconds Johnson's eyes closed.

"By the time he wakes, the Cardinal will be in the Vatican. Wheels up in twenty minutes, gentlemen, let's get going."

The four of them lifted Johnson into the packing crate, nailed the lid on and took it to the van parked at the rear of the building.

***

Mark sat on the sofa in the corner of his hotel room with a full glass of water in one hand and Marion's hand in the other. She had been sitting with him for nearly an hour while everyone else was slumped in opposing corners. No one wanted to talk.

He had been staring at Rebecca's lifeless corpse stretched out on the bed.

Slowly his face filled with rage. At last, it was too much.

"Why didn't you stop her?" he shouted.

The sudden noise stopped everyone.

"Mark, there was nothing we…"

"Mom, there is always something you can do."

Arsalan looked over. "No, Mark, sometimes things happen. I had to learn that from Paul. He saved me and I feel guilty; now Rebecca has saved you."

"And you are missing one small point; Bill abandoned us. As soon as it got tough, he left to play with some of his other pets in another universe. You heard what he said a few days ago. We are nothing to him, a blink in existence. He showed that tonight, and it cost Rebecca her life."

"Mark," said Marion, "it's not Bill's fault."

"Crap!" shouted Mark, and the glass exploded on the wall as he threw it across the room. If it's not God's fault, whose is it? He has got away innocent for too long. Babies die staving, and 'it's God mysterious ways'. A tsunami wipes out a whole town, and we are not supposed to question his judgement. Well, I do judge it, and it's crap." He stormed out of the room.

Marion got up to follow.

Sarah caught her arm. "Let him go. He needs some time."

Marion nodded and sat back on the sofa.

Mark took the elevator to the street. The cool air filled his lungs and he felt he had breathed for the first time since Rebecca…

…died.

Across the road, several hundred people were gathered
underneath a large digital billboard showing scenes all
from over the world. Headlines from governments
condemning the alien imposter scrolled across the
screen. People were seen marching in Asia, Russia, The
Middle East and America. The one thing they had in
common were placards with a likeness of Bill hanging
from a gallows.

A Breaking News banner popped up. 'World marches
to reclaim its religions."

Mark stopped and watched.

"They've actually gone nuts. For thousands of years
they have all been waiting for God to return and, now
he has, they don't like it because he isn't in the same
religion as them."

A woman at the back turned away from the screen for
a moment and noticed him standing across the street
wide-eyed. Something looked familiar to her. Was he
from work?

Mark watched her expression slowly change as she
followed a trail of breadcrumbs around her memories.
Then her mouth opened. Her hand pointed directly at
him and she screamed. "It's him, it's one of the alien's
accomplices."

In unison, every face turned towards him. For a
second, no one moved.

"Sod it!" said Mark and bolted for the doors. A roar
went up behind him, and the crowd ran forward on
mass.

Inside he pressed each of the elevator buttons, and
both doors slid open. He jumped into one and pressed
a floor above his, then he jumped out and did the
same in the other. This time he stayed inside. As the
mob burst into the building, both elevators closed and
started their ascent.

Mark looked around. On the sidewall was a small picture frame containing tonight's menu in the restaurant. He ripped it off and, as the doors opened, dropped it on the floor to stop them from shutting. Next to him, the other elevator was about to close. He quickly jammed his boot in, and they opened again. Grabbing the other menu frame, he did the same to this one. As he ran for the staircase, he heard them both clanking against the doors as they tried to shut. In the lobby, a large crowd had watched the numbers over the top of the elevators going up. Eventually, they both stopped. "22" said the man closest to the buttons. "Got you." He pressed the call button. Nothing happened. Nothing kept happening for a few minutes. "He's Jammed them. Use the stairs."

The crowd ran to the end of the corridor and started up the building.

On floor 22, Mark raced down to the stairwell and then down to his floor.

The rest of the group were still sitting around when he burst in. "We have a problem. Let's move!" and ran back down the hall.

After a quick glance at each other, they ran after him. At the emergency door, he shushed them. "Quiet," he whispered.

After about a minute, dozens of footsteps walked past the door and kept going up. Mark guessed they had started at a run, but after ten storeys, they would have been reduced to a slow jog. By now, they would be getting tired and had changed down to first gear.

The rest of the group moved closer so they could hear him without him talking loud.

"We need to barricade the door and then look for another exit. They know we are here, and all of us are now on the endangered species list."

Everyone headed off and started dragging the heaviest items they could find back to the door.

"Wait," whispered Mark, "I think they have all passed." He pressed the catch and it clicked open.

On the other side, the woman who had recognised in the street was leaning against the railing, trying to catch her breath. As soon as she saw Mark's face appear around the door, she opened her mouth to scream. Nothing came out but a wheezy gasp.

"Evening," said Mark, before he slammed the door closed and started piling furniture against the entrance. Just as he finished, they guessed she had caught her breath because the shouting started.

"Mom, go see if there is another way out."

Marion took off down the hall.

Within a minute, loud banging started the other side of the barricade. A minute after that, Marion returned.

"There is another staircase, but I can hear people shouting as they are coming up."

The door opened a crack, and hands started trying to grab at him as he held it in place. "Go," he shouted to the others, "try to get out or hide."

"I'm not leaving you. I gave birth to you and I will stay if I want."

"Me too," Arsalan said, as he stepped forward and started hitting the mobs hands with a wooden leg he had ripped off a chair. "Not that I gave birth to you, I mean, but I am staying."

Ayaan joined him, occasional firing a shot through the door above the mob's heads to slow them down.

Arsalan frowned.

Ayaan held up his hands. "I didn't kill anyone, probably."

Caroline grabbed Sarah and kissed her hard on the lips. When it finished, she looked her friend in the eyes. "I love you. I knew it the first time we met."

Sarah's eyes filled will tears. "I love you too," she said, and both of them launched themselves at the door to help Mark.

A minute later, it was still stalemate. The mob had not got in and the barricade was holding. "I think we can handle this," said Mark, just as they heard a faint ding thirty feet behind them.

The elevator doors opened and about thirty people carrying bats, knives and guns stepped into the corridor and started to close the distance.

Mark stepped forward. "I think you should know you will have probably exceeded the maximum capacity of those elevators."

The people ignored him and carried on slowly approaching.

He turned back for a second. "Sorry guys, I wish this had a better ending." Suddenly he spun back to the mob and ran headlong at them.

Several guns raised and the hall filled with explosions. But Mark was still standing. They had missed.

The people with guns couldn't believe it. They fired again. Every bullet hit fresh air. One man walked up to Mark and unloaded a clip at point-blank range, and all he hit was a plant pot standing by the wall.

Mark pulled back his fist to throw a punch but stopped mid-air.

He could see the crowd slowly parting at the rear like Moses had arrived, and the mob were the Red Sea.

At last, there were just a few people at the front who had turned to look behind them. Whatever it was, was small. Eventually, they stepped aside and, as they parted, something glowing bright red stepped between them and came into view.

Rebecca's bare feet floated a few inches off of the ground, silently carrying the rest of her towards him.

Her eyes were clear, and she shone like a star. There was not a mark on her.

"Miss me?" she said as she landed gently on the ground in front of him.

He nodded, unable to speak. "Bill? Did he..?"

"No, not Bill, someone else." she held his hand and placed the palm on her stomach. "The girls in our family are natural healers. She brought me back somehow."

It took a few seconds before Mark worked it out. "But when?"

"Yesterday afternoon. You must have managed it between the screams," she kissed him and he hoped she would never stop.

Caroline tapped them both on the shoulders. "Lovely to see you Rebecca, really glad for you both but we still have a problem."

The crowd had started moving towards them again. Rebecca turned around. Her voice seemed to come from all directions.

"I have been thinking about the problem we have, and I believe we need a different perspective to understand what we are facing as a race. So maybe this will help."

Suddenly it was dark and the ground felt unstable without any reference points. Just enough so everyone in the crowd reached out and grabbed someone else's hand in the darkness.

Slowly, a light appeared in the distance and highlighted a gentle curve in the distance. Gradually, the light increased, and people suddenly realised where they were. The moon's surface spread out around them. The faint light got brighter, and eventually, the Earth appeared over the horizon.

Mark leant down to her ear. "Are we really…"

"Yep."

"Bill?"

"You keep crediting Bill with everything. No, this is all me. Impressed?"

"Er yeah. How come we can breathe?"

"Don't ask, it's above your pay grade," she said, cuddling up to him.

Around them, more and more people started appearing. Eventually, on a piece of the moon not a lot bigger than England, the whole human race stood shoulder to shoulder, staring at the little blue, green and white planet in front of them. It looked about the size of a basketball.

Sarah's voice shook the ground they stood on. "Our world now. From here, you cannot see any tribes, boarders or classes. It is just our home."

Suddenly the white snow-covered caps disappeared. "Our home in twenty years."

The blue waters expanded, and the green forests receded. "Here she is again in thirty years."

Clouds filled the skies. They were so thick the planet looked like a giant fluffy ball. Then they cleared.

The surface was brown. No green showed at all. "Forty years."

Then the white appeared at the caps and raced towards the equator. "Fifty years."

Eventually, the ice receded, and the green returned. "One thousand years from now, she will recover, and our race will have been dead for all of them. We can choose to die together or live together, it's up to all of us."

Suddenly, everyone but their original group disappeared.

Arsalan, Ayaan, Carline, Sarah, Marion and Millie bounced through the low gravity towards Rebecca and Mark.

"Nice touch, bringing them to the moon. 'A new perspective'. I like it. Clever. Must be in the genes."

Everyone turned around as Bill strolled up, holding a soccer ball. "Anyone fancy a kick-about before we leave?"

They all shrugged, and he ceremoniously handed the ball to Rebecca. He smiled, "All yours now. I knew you just needed a nudge in the right direction to realise your potential." She looked at the ball in her hands. Instead of team colours, it was an exact likeness of Earth.

She hugged him and then winked. "I'll do my best to look after it."

She turned around, dropped the ball and kicked it as hard as she could into the air. Earth landed a quarter of a mile away, and they all started bouncing towards it.

TWENTY FOUR
(Hours Later)

Angela straightened her Hooters t-shirt. Usually, their customers were very well behaved with good manners, kind hearts and exceptional politeness towards the waitresses, but today she had been dealing with idiots all morning. One middle-aged 90's throwback had palmed her a twenty dollar bill with his phone number written on it.

She looked at it and then at 'Mr shoulder-pads and Cuban lifts'.

"Honey, is this a phone number or your age?" she said, before she walked to the next table. Behind her, the rest of the group howled with laughter.

As she walked away, she saw Bill sitting at the following table, smiling at her.

Angela threw her hands in the air and ran over.

"Hi Angela, how are…"

Angela grabbed Bill, pulled him to his feet and kissed him on the lips. "I didn't think you would come back after your TV interview."

Bill took a second to recover, and then he hugged her. "Angela, wild horses couldn't keep me away from you, your wings and a Pabst. But mostly you."

"I'm sorry," she said. Life has gone crazy here, and I blame you."

"Everyone blames me. Floods, plagues… …you know… …the usual.

238

"No, Bill, my life has *completely* changed for the better. At the end of this week, I have been asked to take over all customer services and sustainability training for our company. And I get a bonus!"

Bill held her hand. "That sounds great."

"Great? I can give up my other two jobs, buy a house in a nice neighbourhood and put my daughter through university."

"So, what are you going to do with the bonus?"

"I have started a website to teach people how to go carbon negative. How amazing is that? I get to teach people to save our planet!"

Angela started to walk away, but Bill said, "Don't you want to know our order?"

"No, I don't think so; I am guessing it's three portions of hot wings and a couple of Pabst for each of you."

Rebecca said, "Beers for the boys, water for the lady with the baby."

"Congratulations, honey," said Angela, and she sashayed towards the bar.

"Angela?" Mark called.

"Yes honey."

"What is your daughter's name?"

"It's Rebecca."

He looked at Bill and then back to Angela. "Of course it is; I bet she's lovely."

"Yes, yes she is an angel in fact." She turned to the bar and placed the order.

Mark leant towards Bill, "Were you something to do with that?"

"Anyway," said Bill, ignoring the question, "what are you two going to do now?"

Rebecca looked over Bill's head. "I was going to help keep things moving in the right direction, but I think I am surplus to requirement." She nodded toward the screen on the wall.

The TV had switched to the news channel. A picture of several figures appeared, each hugging and waving. Over their heads the text read, 'Cleric and Pope lead religions from around the world to welcome a new future for the planet.'

"Looks like my role is redundant," said Rebecca.

Angela arrived with the drinks and put them on the table.

After she left, Mark picked up his bottle and clinked it against Rebecca's and Bill's.

"So, what about you, Bill? What are you going to do?"

"I guess I will carry on visiting different races and help them stay on track as best I can."

"Bill," asked Rebecca, "who made you?"

He thought for a while. "I don't know. Over a few millennia, I remember becoming self-aware. Then I sort of floated around for a while, I'm not really sure how long. Eventually, I decided I needed a hobby and started the great expansion. After I made your universe, I got a bit carried away and made one a week for a couple of hundred years. Suddenly I got swamped juggling all those balls."

Rebecca put her arm around his shoulder. "You must have been lonely until life started evolving. Didn't you ever wonder where you came from?"

Bill took a drink from his beer. "Yes, occasionally I did but, to be honest, you and the other species kept me busy.

"Perhaps you should take some 'me time'," said Mark, handing Bill another Pabst. "You know, have a road trip, go looking for some answers about yourself."

Bill stared at the Pabst for a long time. "Really? You think I could do that? Just think about me for a while and maybe get some answers?"

Rebecca squeezed his shoulder, "Why not? You being around hasn't stopped us screwing up continuously. What else could go wrong?"

"You are right," said Bill. "You guys make a mess of things, even if I am around. I might as well take a few days off."

"There you go." Mark drank his second beer and waved at Angela. He made a circular gesture with his hand to indicate another round.

"Take some time, kick back, find out about your roots." Bill nodded. "Ok I will." Then he paused for a second. "Do you two fancy coming with me?"

"Er, Bill, I'm having a baby. Is prehistory a good place for a pregnant woman?"

"And you think Miami is better?"

Angela arrived with the food.

Mark, Bill and Rebecca swapped glances.

"Angela," said Rebecca standing up, "can we get these to go? Looks like we will be eating on the road."

The end.

ABOUT THE AUTHOR

Jack East spent most of his formative years in London and, even though life enabled him to travel the world, he still regards it as home.

He lives by a simple creed.

"Ok, its impossible,
now, how do we do it."

www.jackeastbooks.com

Printed in Great Britain
by Amazon

22112571R00138